# The Devil's Gunt

By Gerald Dean Rice

Kindle Edition

**Other titles available on Kindle…**

*Dead 'til Dawn*

*Absolute Garbage, Total Nonsense, & Utter*

*Ridiculousness*

**Pre-order now!**

*a lowercase hell*

Gerald Dean Rice

# a lowercase hell

# The Devil's Gunt

Gerald Dean Rice

## Prologue: The White Man

He came at the rear of a caravan about thirty carriages long. Everybody stop workin', even Boss held his whip to look. Ma'am Davies even dragged her fat self out the house to come see.

She looked scared. While people was watchin' 'nem carriages I was watchin' Ma'am Davies. Well, mo' specific her daughter Isis, but it wasn't possible to look anywhere in the missus' direction and not see Ma'am Davies.

Isis was the prettiest girl on alla Cannonade Plantation but that ain't why I like her. She taught me how to read and teachin' me how to speak proper 'cause she want me to run away with her to Paris or England. At least she say.

"What they speak over there?" I asked her. And, "They got niggas over there too?" She gimme a different answer every time but I don't care. I ain't goin' nowhere with Isis. I'mma learn good from her so when I run away I can get a job usin' my brain.

Or maybe one of these carriages might take me away. . .

All the carriages line up right in front of the house. Ma'am Davies and all her chirrun line up with all the servants just behind. Every carriage is the finest I ever saw and everyone got two white horses with a patch of black right on they foreheads. That's sixty horses that all look just alike. I figure a

1

man gotta be pretty rich to be able to find that many horses that look the same.

For the longest time nobody moved. I thought I was the onliest one lookin' at anything not connected to a horse (lessen you count Isis' momma) and then a door to the last carriage opened.

All my life I been around white folk. French, German, Irish, even a couple Jews, but I ain't never seen somebody *this* white. He was as pale as Mister Davies after he slit his own throat out back of the house. I found him and the note he left. I knew some of my words back then and could make out a little but I gave it straight to Sara who really couldn't read and she gave it to the missus.

Mister Davies had always been a strange one and M'dear told us all not to have no hot tongue or we'd get a tanned hide but we all knew. Mister Davies liked sneakin' down to the slave quarters after midnight. We all guessed he just couldn't live with his self no mo'.

But this white man was strange beyond his milk-white skin. He was all wrapped up in white scarves from toe to tip like he fell out the tallest oak tree he could find and somebody bound him up 'cause every part of him was broke. But he was tall and moved like an October deer, weaving between the carriages until he was nose up with Ma'am Davies.

She was higher than she was wide but there was something about him that made her seem small. She smiled like she knew him but she seemed

2

nervous some. Not at all like the woman who'd overseen more than one nigga get whipped to death.

The white man turned away and started for the field where we was. Now all of a sudden we got back to work. My hands was as hard as any man's but quicker. By the time he got to us I'd filled my sack and needed another. I was good for at least two hundred fifty pounds in a day. I dropped off my sack and was gettin' another from the Boss when the white man came upon me, whiter than I'd first thought he was. It hurt my eyes to look at him in the sun and so I looked down at his feet.

I could feel his eyes on me and Boss beside me shifting back and forth like a drunk three-legged cat.

"You get back on back to work!" Boss said and I flinched when he motioned with his whip like he was about to lash me. The white man was lookin' at me and stepped close enough. Boss wouldda hit either one of us. I couldn't help but look up at him too, hopin' he wasn't lookin' at me like Mister Davies sometimes did. He picked up my arm by the wrist—his hands was huge—between his pointer finger and thumb, delicate as a butterfly.

"Look at me." His voice was high like a girl's.

I took my time, afraid to obey and afraid not to. His eyes beneath that big hat looked some shade a' purple. He smiled and the little bit a' teeth I could see looked…sharp.

"Come."

He pulled me along behind him like he knew where he was goin'. I could barely keep up. I was tall for ten but I was still a skinny boy and he was a grown man. Several people followed behind and I didn't have the guts to see who, afraid Ma'am Davies would be takin' note of what I was doin' and decidin' how to punish me later.

We stopped in a clearin' and the white man let me go. My sister—not my for-real sister—was bent and pickin' away when she must have heard somethin' that made her straighten up. She turned and looked at us, her baby strapped to her. He wasn't no more than six weeks old, huge brown eyes and skin like dusk. The white man clapped his hands together once and he smiled big. His teeth looked like normal teeth now as he came close.

"May I?" he asked Shanti. She looked down, up, at me, confused as any of us. Wasn't none of us used to bein' asked nothin' by white folk. Then she nodded and took the baby out the papoose. She held him out, naked as when he was born and the white man took him. He held the boy up, smilin' at him like he was his own child. Then he held him to his breast and turned for all of us to see him holdin' the baby.

Ma'am Davies was there then and to my surprise, she held a hand up in front of me like she was guardin' me from this man.

"*Cissy*," he said. "This baby is *beautiful*."

"Yessir. He is," she said.

He cooed to the baby, suckling his finger. I hadn't been around the chap too much on account of him bein' so colicky but he was quiet. He was *smilin'*.

"Take care of this child," he said. He looked up from the baby to Ma'am Davies. "Remove any obstacle. For his life whole."

The white man came close to Ma'am Davies who was still holdin' her hand up in front of me. His eyes danced in his head as he handed the baby over.

"Yessir." She wrapped a protective arm around him.

"Feed him."

"I will. He'll only have the best."

"Feed him. Now."

"I...absolutely."

He turned them purple eyes on me.

"Watch."

I opened my mouth but I didn't dare speak. I watched Ma'am Davies tug out one a' them mighty ole tits right in front a' everyone but only the white man and me watchin'. She had to pin the bulk of that tit to her chest with a hand to keep from smotherin' the baby as it fastened onto her nipple.

She made a sound that was half laugh, half cry as the baby began to suckle.

"Boy," he said to me. "You will keep watch. His whole life."

## Chapter 1. Immaculate Conniption

Median hooked her leg like he was pinning her for a count of three. He stroked her like a well-oiled machine and she was moaning like she was really into it.

"Turn over," the director said behind him. He got on his knees and Mariah flipped. He was surprised he was even here. Median was a last minute replacement after Chad Boy had broken his penis on a shoot in Tijuana. Mariah had been around long enough to command who her co-workers were and was now producing most of her stuff when she stepped in front of the camera.

"Oo-oo-oo!" she said and he knew he had her. She always moaned like that when she climaxed for real. At least that's what Gary Gold told him once. He continued hammering away, pulling at her hips until she started queefing with each stroke.

Median had started sweating from the lights beating down on them. He swiped his brow and noted the tiny pool of sweat jiggling in the small of her back with each stroke.

Mariah popped her middle fingers in and out of her mouth and reached under to lube herself. Her long fingernails jabbed the base of his cock but he kind of liked it.

"Pull my hair! Squeeze my tits!" she commanded and he obeyed. She was only looking out for him because he probably looked like an automaton pistoning into her.

"Okay, Mariah, I want him to get over you with your legs spread and you on your head."

Median knew the position and he got in place. It was the pile driver, probably his specialty because he was particularly good at bending his erect penis.

He thought he was getting into a groove but the director called for missionary again a few minutes into it. Median found himself noticing the crow's feet at the corners of Mariah's eyes and wondered how old she was. He had figured early thirties but now had the sensation he might have been off by a decade at least.

Mariah sank her fingernails into his butt, reminding him to moan and he complied. He put one of her legs up on his chest and licked her calf. He was just about to palm her hips when something pinched him.

At first it was only slight and was right in the entrance to his butthole. He thought it might have been some kind of cramp and ignored it but then the pain intensified and deepened, penetrating him up to his lower intestine.

Median screamed and his hips pumped as he began to cum. He was able to withdraw but that made it worse. He spooged on Mariah's chest, coating her in thick ropes the likes of which even Peter North had never shot. He turned away as his penis continued, his lower body jerking as more goo jetted out of him.

"Hey, get back over there!" the director said. Median spaz-walked in his direction, intending to ask for help.

"Ugh-ugh-ughhhhhhhh!" he said as semen arced out of him, splashing onto the director's pants and the shoes of a few crew members standing behind him.

But he'd only begun his orgasm, the contractions becoming more and more intense as he blasted farther and farther, hitting more people behind the camera and the cameras too.

The pinching inside his ass intensified, nothing about this orgasm being pleasurable as he moaned in high-pitched horror.

Patty the Fluffer and Oswaldo ran over to him but Median painted them both. He finally dropped to his knees hoping to aim away from anybody but constricting blood flow to his legs only made it worse.

Gouts of jizz shot skyward only to rain down on people standing around. The boom guy, the best boy, the caterers (and the food), the assistant director, and a woman who had just snuck in to watch.

People started running aimlessly, many colliding with each other, slipping and falling, getting trampled, or getting their eyes stung with exhaustive helpings of man mayo.

Median finally collapsed from exhaustion, emptier than he'd ever felt in his life. Mariah carefully made her way over to him, slipping but managing not to fall.

"Honey, are you okay?"

Median heard her but he could hardly move. She put a finger on his knee and he was barely able to look in her direction. She was touching what looked to be the only dry spot on his body.

"I…I…my *balls.*" In truth, it was his balls, back, hips, and abdomen, but his balls hurt the worst. The painful ass cramp had ceased. Finally.

Mariah wiped goo out of her eyebrow and smiled at him. He could tell she didn't know what to say. Then the director came over.

"You're fired. Get the fuck out of here. *Now*."

He turned and left, swearing up a storm as he went.

"It'll all work out," Mariah said. "I'm sure of it."

## Chapter 2 - Something Something...Something Something Just Ain't Right

The alarm clock went off, blaring a Keith sweat tune he recognized from long ago.

Median sat slowly up in bed. He felt like crap, figuring that must've been because of yesterday. After he was finally strong enough to leave the set he had been thirsty all day long. He thanked god he'd been able to get a shower in before the director threw him out. Mariah had gone to bat for him for some reason, deflecting most of the man's anger.

He figured he might've been coming down with something. Yesterday probably had taxed his immune system and he had come in contact with somebody who had been sick. A cold. By this time next week he would probably be right as rain again.

Median jerked out of bed and ran for the bathroom. He'd begun heaving, mentally demanding his stomach to settle but he was past the point of whether or not he was going to hurl. This was going to happen.

He tried to turn the door knob but it was locked.

"Oc*upado*!" Joe said from inside.

Median asked as politely as he could for his roommate to exit so he could use the facilities. But it came out like, "GefuggoutIneedtothorp!"

"What are you doing out there?" Joe asked. "I'm mid-shit."

Median continued blowing chunks, reminiscent of the low point of his day just twelve hours ago. He definitely had not eaten this much and didn't understand where this…*material* was coming from. He was still weak and slowly collapsed in his newly made puddle.

The toilet flushed a moment later and Joe came out.

"What are you doing out here? Oh, man, gross!"

Median wasn't unconscious but he didn't have the strength to move around a whole lot. He would have liked to have made the argument that the smell coming from the bathroom wasn't a hell of a lot better.

A moment later a towel dropped over him and then Joe was dragging him. When he opened his eyes again he saw he was somewhere near the nook table by the kitchen. Median and Joe lived in a one bedroom apartment, Median taking the pull-out couch while Joe had the bedroom. They'd decided who got the bedroom with a best of seventeen game of paper, rock, scissors that Median suspected had been rigged against him.

By the time Median came to again Joe was dressed and looked like he was heading out.

"I gotta see a lady about a boat," he said on his way out.

Median got to his hands and knees, still feeling shaky. His chest was sore and his head was starting to pound. He was able to push through cleaning up the mess he'd made before he found two pills rattling around in a bottle of aspirin. He swallowed them with a couple handfuls of water from the sink, grimacing from the vomit aftertaste.

His stomach grumbled. Median turned to the toilet then headed to the kitchen after he realized he was hungry. He had some Chinese leftovers from a couple days ago unless Joe had eaten them. He stepped into the tiny kitchen, yanked open the refrigerator door and stared at the human head, staring back at him.

## Chapter 3. - Head's Up

Well, stared at the big box in the refrigerator next to the mustard. He peeked under the lid, hoping it was a cake.

"Who are you?" the head inside asked him. He'd only seen a forehead and a pair of eyes but he was reasonably certain of the rest.

"Who am I? What the fuck are you doing in my fridge?" Median slammed the door in the head's face and stared at it, willing the unwelcome contents inside to disappear. He'd seen strange things in the refrigerator before in the middle of the night and they were always gone by morning.

"Hey! Hey!" the head shouted. "Are you out there?"

"No," Median said.

"Well then I'm talking to whoever is out there not named Joe."

Median figured this was no ordinary hallucination. It knew his friend's name. He opened the door again.

"How did you get in there?"

"Well, that's a simple and a difficult question to answer. The real noodle-bender is how I'm talking right now."

Median just stared at it.

"You look real skeptical right now. What if I told you a couple things to prove I'm on the up-and-up?"

"Go ahead," Median said after a long moment.

"Your name is Walker Median Harris. Parents are Martha and Earl. You have a half-sister, Carmen—"

"I don't have a sister. My parents have been married since high school. I'm an only child."

"Wait-wait-wait!" the head said before he shut the door again. "You probably want to call your father. Your parents live in Tucson, right?"

"Okay, I must be hallucinating. Yes, my parents live in Tucson. I know that and that's why *you* know that."

"But you don't know about your sister."

"I don't have a—"

"Call your father. Speak to him alone. Ask him about the townhouse by 75 in Detroit. Once you know, then I can tell you the really freaky stuff."

"Okay, goodbye."

Median shut the door and walked over to the couch. He was feeling better despite his weak stomach. He folded the mattress back in and reset the pillows. Eleven in the morning and it was already a helluva day. He thought about calling his folks. If his hallucination was telling him to call that could be sign enough. He didn't believe the sister thing, that was ridiculous, but it had been a while since he'd called.

"Nah." He wasn't going to call because his imagination told him to. Besides, what would he say?

'Mom, Dad, a decapitated head told me to pick up the phone and ask if I have a bastard sister.'

Silly.

Although. . .

Wasn't there a time when he was little when his father had been gone a long time? He still came around a lot but Median specifically remembered his father not staying overnight. His parents would both put him to bed, like it was some sort of weird competition. She'd tuck him in, then he would redo the covers. He'd read a bedtime story and then she'd read one and do all the voices.

It had really scared him for a while. Like his parents weren't really his parents, like in that movie he saw. He'd stay awake for hours after, certain they were going to come back and eat him or something.

And when his father's car started and he heard him drive away, Median had been certain the danger had been averted.

He picked up the phone and dialed.

"Hello?" his mother said, picking up on the first ring.

"Oh, hey, Ma, how are you?"

"Walker? Is that you? It's not my birthday."

"I know. I just…was thinking about you. I wanted to call to say 'hi'. Hi."

"What's wrong?"

"Nothing. Well, I woke up a little sick this morning."

"Sick? Have you been sitting on farm equipment again?"

"Oh, no. Nothing like that." He'd caught VD when he was sixteen and had heard someone say they had told their parents they'd gotten it from riding on a thresher. He'd told his parents that even though they lived in midtown Detroit. "Just a cold. It's really kicking my butt."

"*Language.*"

"*Bottom.* Sorry, Mama."

She waited a beat and said, "So, it's just a cold?"

*Just a cold?* he thought. *Since when was a cold ever just a cold?*

His mother had always made the biggest deal out of anything going wrong with him. It was upsetting that it sounded like she was just blowing it off.

15

He considered telling her what really was going on but if he told too much he might wind up telling her about yesterday. So far as his mother was concerned he was still virginal, waiting for the right girl to make his wife.

"Yeah. It's just a cold."

There was something odd about her tone too. Almost like she was distracted. Then something electric started. Median thought it was a blender.

"You making a cake?" he asked.

"What? Uh, yeah. Mm, chocolate."

"Oo, I'd like some. Maybe I'll swing by."

"No! You're not in Arizona, are you?"

He was kidding and thought it was obvious but what was going on? He'd never been not welcomed at his parents' home. He wanted to ask what was going on.

"Is Daddy there?" Median knew he was. His father never went anywhere.

"He's uh…he's uh…in the bathroom. You know him. He'll be in there all day."

His father had always bragged how he'd been regular since 1982. Once at six in the morning and again at seven in the evening. It was almost noon.

"Mama, is everything okay over there? Do you need me to come down?"

"Oh, no, sweetie. Everything's fine. Your father and I just have some plans, is all. He had to use the bathroom before we got started—I mean before we go out. Did you need something, baby?"

"I just wanted to speak to Daddy. It can wait. I'll just call later."

"Nonsense. Whatever you wanted to ask him you can ask me. There's no advice better than Mama's."

It was too late to back out. But maybe he could hedge a little. "Remember when I was little? When Daddy was gone a lot? Why was he gone so much?"

"Well, your father was in sales. Sometimes he had to travel overnight." The blender-sounding thing revved a couple times.

"I remember he was in sales. That was when I was in high school. I mean before that."

"Hm. Before that? I don't remember. I mean maybe he needed to be away from home a time or two."

"No. This was longer than that. Like, months straight."

Mama was silent a long moment. "There was a time…when your father had to leave. . ." Her voice was very controlled, like the sound a teapot makes right before it whistles. "His *mother* was ill. Very ill, god rest her soul."

"But Ma, Nana passed when I was a sophomore—"

"She was very *ill*." Her voice cracked. "Your father took care of her until she died. That is the end of the story. Understand?"

"Yes, Ma'am." It was a lie and they both knew it. His father's mother was in the peak of health for a woman in her seventies. She'd died in a skiing accident—

"Is there anything more?" she asked, her voice more composed.

"No, Ma'am."

"Good. I look forward to talking to you on my birthday. I love you, dear."

"I love you too, Mama." He heard the clinking of the phone as it was placed halfway back into the cradle.

There was a giant *whoosh* of a toilet flush and then his father said somewhere in the background, "I'm ready for my medicine," in a singsong voice.

There was the *stretch-slap* of something rubber and then the blender-thing came on again. *Full bore.*

"Ooo," his father said. His mother giggled like a schoolgirl.

"You ready?"

Before he could answer the sound of the blender-thing changed. Bogged down. Like it was blending particularly *thick* batter.

Median disconnected the call. To avoid the images in his mind attempting to fill the gaps of what was going on in his parents' home three thousand miles away he stormed into the kitchen, threw the refrigerator door open and took the box out. He sat it on the counter and popped the lid off, tossing it away.

"What do you know?" he asked the decapitated head.

"No, what do *you* know? Did he tell you about your sister?"

Median thought about clapping the lid back on the box, marching it to the dumpster, and tossing it in but he knew he'd just be right back seventeen minutes later, up to his knees in garbage, fishing it out again.

"In a way," he said. "Let's just say I won't be eating my mother's German chocolate cake anytime soon."

The head tried to nod but only succeeded in tipping itself over. Before he realized he'd done it, Median sat it upright again.

"Now that we got one baffling thing out the way I'm going to need you to pack a bag so we can get out of here."

"We? Why are we going anywhere?"

"Two reasons. One, you're pregnant with the devil's baby and two, Joe is probably on his way back to add me to his creepy collection of body parts."

## **Chapter 4. Hammercock!**

"This man," the angel says pointing at the man in the photo and locking eyebones with me. "I need you to bring him to me unharmed. Do we have an agreement?"

"What is a man if not for his word?" I say and stare off in the distance. There's a million miles between me and somewhere but I got no better place to be.

"I'm sorry, I need a simple yes or no, Mr. Hammercock."

"Simple yeah. I'll bring you your stooge," I say. "Right side up."

He drops four heavy gold coins in my mitt. I almost ask him for another for the pain it'll be to fence 'em but I nod and go my way. I'm a big guy but the angel is bigger. At least two and a half bills despite the pretty green eyes and the pouty lips. He has the kind of face you'd buy a drink you could slip a mickey in if he wasn't looking.

I was in the lowlife game and I'd tracked down more than my share. This Walker Harris was gonna be a cakewalk. A loner's loner who swam in smut and looked like he had lost his way home. I'd seen a thousand just like him. Maybe I'd impress the angel and he would let me buy him a burger and a brew. Maybe I'd take him home and he'd take me to heaven.

"That's a tall order," I say aloud, talking myself down from a cloud. Mere mortals like me never get the gold, silver, or bronze. We just get the certificate of participation and use it to slit our wrists, praying to be let out of the game.

I have to keep it in my hat where it belongs. Easy or not, this job has some sharp corners that'll cut if I don't pay attention to how I turn. An angel means a devil. So long as I don't get on his dance card I'd call myself the luckiest guy on Earth not to come foot to hoof with him.

I clap my hand on my hat, get in the bucket, and crank her up. She coughs then purrs like a kitty with a three pack a day habit. I haven't changed her oil since '87 and don't see reason to break the streak. She's my lucky ride and I'm taking her all the way.

This Harris character has to be somebody worth killing for if somebody from the other side wants him. I figure for an all-seeing, all-knowing creature to seek me out to do the job he knows my reputation. He knows I don't do so good at witness protection. Then my brains start turning and I realize—he's an angel. Where do you go when you die? Upstairs or downstairs. But the angels oversee all that, don't they? Sorting out who goes in which direction. He has to know what I'm good at and be saying without saying what he wants me to do.

So I have it figured. I kill this guy so he meets his maker ASAP.

## Chapter 5. Rick's Baby

"I'm *what*?" Median asked. Had he not been driving on the freeway he might have picked up the box and shook the head inside.

"You're pregnant," the head said again.

"Now I know you're a figment of my imagination," he said. "I'm a dude."

"Well, considering who the father is, your gender is unimportant."

"All right, I'll bite. Who's the father?"

"The devil. Well, more specifically, *a* devil. His name is Rick."

"Rick the devil impregnated me, huh? Funny, I don't remember sleeping with any demons."

"Not a demon. A *devil*. Big difference."

Median wasn't about to argue whether there was a difference or not. That would have implied him acknowledging he'd been impregnated.

"I'm not pregnant."

The head didn't say anything.

"You hear me?" Median glanced at the top of the head's head in the box.

". . .I hear you."

"And how would you even know, huh? You're just a...a...a head in a box!"

"I actually have an answer for that. I've been thinking."

"Shut up!"

The head didn't say anything.

"Well, go ahead. How would you know?"

"I'm dead. I have a sort of mental screenshot of everything that was happening right at the moment I died."

"So what—you know everything now?"

"No. Just everything that was happening when I died. One of those things being a devil impregnating you."

"You *don't* know that. Stop saying that." Median swerved back into his lane.

It sounded like the head took a deep breath.

"Well?"

"Well what?"

"What do you want me to say here, Median?"

"I don't know. Tell me how likely it is that you're mistaken. Maybe you saw a demon—*devil*—and it wasn't impregnating me at all. Maybe it was somebody else. When did you die?"

The head told him and when Median did some mental subtraction he realized where he was and what probably was happening to him at the time. His rectum was still sore.

"What does any of this mean?" he asked quietly.

"No clue. All I can tell you is what I've seen. But I'm sure if a devil impregnated you he isn't done with you."

Median's face got hot. He cranked down his window and let the air blow in, the change in pressure pounding at his eardrums.

Then he threw up.

"Okay, I'm hungry," he said.

"Now?" the head said. "You just—"

Median threw up again.

"—just—"

And again.

"—I'm going to be sick—"

And again.

The head was still dry heaving by the time Median had regained his composure.

"I need something to eat."

"Oh my god!" The head began making more sick sounds.

Median pulled off the freeway and turned into the first fast food place they came to. He'd never heard of the Telway and saw they didn't have a drive-thru but once he smelled the place he knew he was going in.

"You wait here. I'll only be a few minutes."

"Is that a joke?" the head asked as he shut the door.

Median followed a man into a small alcove area inside the restaurant. There was a small window where the bald man placed his order with a

dour-looking thin woman with dual ponytails who
looked between twenty-five and forty-five.

The bald man paid for his order and stepped
aside. Median stepped up, the smell even stronger,
and saw through the window tiny square patties and
onions smoking on a grill. Sliders.

"Let me get six with cheese and pickle."

"You want ketchup and mustard?" She
sounded closer to fifty, her voice a rusty saw.

"No mustard."

"Gimme six bloody babies, hold the snot!"
she called over her shoulder. She gave Median the
total and he dug his wallet out of his pocket. His
cell phone came with it and he realized he'd turned
it off at some point yesterday. He paid for his order
and turned it back on. A moment later his cell
dinged, indicating he had a voicemail. He checked
the number and saw it was from the director.
Median was sure he didn't want to hear the
message.

But then his cell began dinging in rapid
succession. Mostly the same number but there were
a couple he didn't recognize. So Walt was angry but
he certainly wouldn't have left multiple messages
yelling at him. When the cell stopped he had almost
twenty messages, the most recent one received
about fifteen minutes ago.

Median took the white bag from the woman
when his order was ready. Already grease was
turning the corners of the bag translucent. He got in
the car as he was checking his voicemail.

"You motherfucker!" Walt was shouting. "You will never work—you'll be lucky—*FUCK YOU!*"

Median deleted that one and listened to the next. "You got me in the eye, you sonnova—"
*Delete.*

He hoped they weren't all like this and skipped to the last one.

"Okay-okay. I'm sorry. I should *not* have gone off like that. Just call me, okay? I already paid you for yesterday. Check for yourself and call me, okay? *Please.*"

*Please?*

Since when was Walt Wimmer a 'please' sort of guy? He'd gotten a compound fracture in a car accident a decade ago and rumor had it he'd been conscious through his leg being reset because he didn't want to ask to be put out.

Something was definitely odd and Median wasn't so sure he wanted to find out what.

"Was that Walt Wimmer?" the head asked.

Median gasped. He'd forgotten the head was there.

"Yeah. He wants me to call him."

"Figures."

Median turned to the head. "What do you mean 'figures'?"

The head made a face like it was shrugging without shoulders.

"Think about it. You blasted off for like thirty seconds straight. You ever see that in porn before?"

"No." Median thought a moment. "You don't think he wants me to do it again, do you?"

"A one-man bukkake machine. You tell me."

"Holy shit." Median started the car.

"Do you think you could?"

"I didn't know I could do it the first time."

"Where are we going, by the way?"

"To see Mariah Moore. I was thinking maybe she could help me sort some of this out."

## Chapter 6. - Load Dropper

They pulled up in front of her house and parked. Median worked out a sliver of onion beneath his fingernail with his teeth. He was full but wished he'd gotten more. He knew he was going to be hungry again soon. The head thought they'd smelled good too and had asked for him to wave one under his nose. He'd almost done it until he remembered the head, though it talked through some magical means, was dead.

"So what's our plan?" the head asked.

"What do you mean?" Median said. "I'm just gonna go in and talk to her. You're going to stay here."

"I know you're going to talk to her." the head rolled its eyes. "What are you going to *ask* her?"

Median didn't know what to say.

"You don't know what to ask her, do you?"

"Yes. Yes, I do."

The head made a face at him and Median realized it was looking for him to tell it exactly what.

"Okay. What do I ask her?"

"Well, for starters, you can't just come out and accuse her. Usually with these bargains with the devil somebody has signed a contract to get something in exchange. When you get in, look around. Try to figure out what she may have gotten. But be cool with it. Be circumspect. Talk to her about other stuff too."

"Like what?"

"Do I know her or do you know her? What kinds of things do you talk about with people you know? Hell, seduce her for all I care. You already slept with her."

"We didn't sleep."

"I know what you did. And you know what I mean. Get in there and pump her for information. Even if you have to pump her!"

Median got out the car. Before he shut the door he peeked back in to put the lid back on. "Why are you helping me?" he asked the head.

"I'm doomed," the head said. Median blinked like he didn't understand. "I mean it. Your roommate didn't kill me by chance. He stalked me. I was a bad person. I look at…this as sort of a grace period. If I can stop a devil from doing whatever it is he's trying to do maybe I can go to the slightly better place."

Median laughed. "What, do you mean heaven?"

"Oh, no, I can't get in there. It's too exclusive. But there are gradations of afterlife between heaven and hell. If I can wind up on the better side I'll take it. Heaven is full of Mormons anyway."

"Mormons, for real? So they were right?"

"I wouldn't say right so much as more insistent than anybody else. After a certain amount of them got there everybody else started leaving."

"Leave? How do you *leave* heaven?"

"Blaspheme, I guess. I'd think you could leave anytime you want. Otherwise, heaven is a prison, right?"

"Oh. Okay." Median shut the door and began walking up the walkway to Mariah's front door. He tried thinking up a conversation starter, something that would put her at ease when she saw him. He had only been to her house one other time for a party and he hadn't exactly felt welcomed to come back.

He was midway up her walkway when he looked up and saw her standing in the doorway. Crap. He smiled, his mind spinning for something to say.

"You're here because you got the devil's seed in you, right?"

"Uh, yeah," he said.

He stopped at the steps to the small porch. Mariah took a long drag off a cigarette, then flicked it away, unfinished.

"Come on."

She was already on her couch, another cigarette in hand, a drink in the other by the time he shut the door.

"So what do you want to know?" she asked.

"I want to know everything." Median shut the door behind him. "How? Why? What can I do to stop it?"

"Well the first one is a bit of a broad question and I don't think we have time enough for the answer." She sucked on her cigarette and blew out smoke. "Why don't I tell you how I am involved?"

"Okay," Median said.

"Median, do you know how old I am?"

He felt like the question was a test. Median was thirty-five and he guessed she was a few years younger than him and she had been in the industry for at least fifteen years. She had the tiniest hint of crow's feet at the corners of her eyes but everything about her was young and athletic. She was about five-seven with long, wavy raven hair, shapely legs with a considerable amount of muscle (she'd squeezed him with her thighs a little tighter than he'd cared for yesterday), a vague six-pack, and an ass that could crack walnuts.

"Don't be shy. I won't be offended." She pointed to a glass on the table. "You're thirsty. Here, have something to drink.

"Thirty," he said, picking up the glass. Median hoped he hadn't upset her. He took a sip then downed the whole glass.

"You're sweet." She smiled and stamped out her cigarette on her coffee table. She had on a silk robe cinched around her waist with an arm folded across her stomach. She didn't seem to have anything on beneath.

"Are you cold?"

She waved him off. "I'm always cold, dear-heart." She lit up another cigarette even though she hadn't finished the last one. Median realized she was nervous. "When I was younger I made a deal with him. I'd get to be in movies that would be seen all over the world. Men and women would love me."

"You sold him your soul?"

She made a face. "Don't be so naive, Median. The devil doesn't want your soul. He gets thousands a day for free—why would he pay anyone anything for theirs?"

"I don't know. Maybe you would have gone to heaven if you hadn't made a deal?"

She rolled her eyes. "Look on the coffee table here. There are two dimes. Quickly tell me which one was minted first."

Median looked down and it took him a couple seconds to even spot the two coins. He was too far away to read anything on them and took a step closer.

"Time's up. It doesn't matter. With the steady influx of souls going into hell nobody has time to see whether or not *one* is special. It's a volume-based business. Quantity over quality. And the place is just about full anyway."

"So. . ."

"So why does the devil make deals?" Mariah took a long drag off her cigarette and held it. "Because there's something else he wants. You ever hear of cap and trade?"

"Isn't that like an emissions thing?"

Mariah nodded, blowing twin plumes of smoke from her nose.

"It's a means of controlling pollution via a central authority that sells a certain number of permits to discharge amounts of different pollutants over a defined amount of time. It's like a buffet except the companies are the customers and they are taking food off their plates."

"I don't think I understand."

"Well, there's more than one devil. I don't know—there are hundreds, maybe thousands. Every one of them is responsible for incoming souls. They have to make room. Sometimes they game the system and do something that isn't strictly legal."

She wiggled her index and middle fingers with the last word. Median continued looking confused.

"There is law after death, Median. The devil—all of them—fudge their numbers everywhere they can. They want to show the numbers of souls under them is increasing but they also have to make room to warehouse all these souls."

All this exposition was making Median's bladder ache. He felt like she was coming to a point but he couldn't wait much longer.

"One of the ways is by sneaking souls *out* of hell." She smiled at him.

"Are…are *you* supposed to be in hell?"

Mariah laughed. "No. I'm very much alive. But I struck my deal with him."

"Could I ask…what did you agree to do for him?"

"I'm a rider." She shook her head, seeing he didn't understand. "I allow souls to ride me. Maybe two or three at a time for a few months. A year at most."

"So…you allow them to possess you?"

"No. I see what you mean, but it's totally different. One, possession is done without permission. And typically with possession the possessed loses control of his or her own body. When you're a rider you allow an extra soul inside you and it's pretty much dormant. You might take on a couple mannerisms that the soul had in life, but you remain in control. Typically, medication keeps you even keel."

"Oh." Median needed a moment to absorb all that. "Could I use your bathroom?"

"Sure. Down the hall on the left. The door is open." Mariah pointed.

Median found the bathroom and half closed the door. He lifted the seat and undid his fly.

"If you want, I can take that out of you," she said from the other room.

"Excuse me?" he said.

"The baby. I can take it out."

He almost asked if she was talking about an abortion but he wasn't a hundred percent accepting his situation.

"Oh, okay."

"Okay?" The door pushed all the way open and there Mariah was with a fresh cigarette. "Okay."

"Aw, man!" He jumped in surprise and splashed a little outside the bowl. Median felt the need to cover up even though he'd had just about every kind of sex possible with this woman. "Almost done here."

"You don't have to be shy with me, cowboy. I know what kind of six-shooter you're packing."

That made him blush and feel stupid at the same time. The emptier Median's bladder got, the more light-headed he became.

"I think I need to sit down," he said, stumbling a little as he shook off, is pants sliding down his thighs. He shook off and bent to flush the toilet and promptly sat in the bathtub.

"Easy," Mariah said. "You don't want to hurt that baby, do you?"

He laughed. "I thought you were going to help me get rid of it?"

"I will." Mariah was suddenly leaning over him, pulling his pants and ankles down. "I'm going to take it out of you and put it in me."

"What?" The edges of Median's vision were going gray. He said something but didn't understand himself and couldn't think of what he was trying to say.

"I know a spell. I haven't perfected it. In fact, I'll more than likely pull all your guts out along with the baby but then I can put it in me. I mean you'll probably die shortly after but won't that be great? You just take a load off and I'll be right with you."

The doorbell rang.

"Shit," she said.

## **Chapter 7. - Her**

She rode him like a queen, isolating her back so only her hips moved. Even her moan with a mouthful of cock was sexy and she still had the presence of mind to jerk the third guy off with a steady, even pace.

Celeste was dirty blonde, petite, with big brown doe eyes. To look at her before the triple team Median would never have guessed she was capable of what she was doing now but she might well have been the best he'd ever seen. He was hard as a rock and he never got an erection at work unless he had a scene coming up.

The director called for a switch to DP and she turned around on the guy she was on top of, riding reverse cowgirl. One of the other guys got in front of her and she made sure she had a good grip on the handjob guy. She was taking all three guys on and didn't seem phased about it at all.

"She on something?" Median asked Corey Clut, the director's assistant.

"No. We chatted a little before start. I offered her a little toot and she said she never touches the stuff."

"She's like…she's like *wow.*"

"I know. She fucks like a fucking angel," Corey said. "She is like wow. You think I don't know she's like wow?" Corey may or may not have been some sort of mobster. He dressed like he was, at least. Well, one from the seventies with his burgundy suits, flared pants, big collars, and open shirts. He smoothed his finger and thumb across his pencil mustache for maybe the fiftieth time and pointed.

"You see that move there?" he asked, referring to a very deliberate way she was moving her hips. "That is something not even seasoned pros know how to do. I'm tellin' you the girl's got it. She can write her own ticket. I'm gonna talk to Ed about a gangbang we got comin' up."

"Not so soon with that, Corey." Median felt a pang of jealousy. "Like you said, she's on her way up. Gangbangs are for burnouts trying to keep their names out there."

"No-no. I got this idea." Corey spread his hands in the air and then made fists like he was snatching his idea from the air. "I can't talk about it yet. But trust me." He kissed his fingertips. "It's gonna be *superb*."

After the scene was over she was all Median could think about. He was absolutely positive he was in love.

She would have gone to the showers and he waited for her outside the door. Maybe he could take her out for a cup of coffee or lunch. He didn't want to fuck her, he wanted to *date* her. He hadn't felt like this about anyone since his wife. Then he thought better of what he was doing and moved a few feet away.

"Hey, M!" Corey called to him from back on the set, waving him over like he was directing traffic. "C'mere!" He was standing by the desk. One of the guys who had been in the scene was still naked but had on a pair of yellow rubber gloves. He was spraying down a spot on the floor and had a sponge in his other hand. Eddie Moneyshot kept a tight budget.

Median didn't want to move. Usually people weren't in too much of a hurry to leave a set but some people had other jobs or a family to get to. So long as Corey didn't take too much time…

"What's up, C?"

"Look." Corey pointed to the desk. Two clear lines of fluid were laid like an X across it. "They crossed streams." He giggled.

The naked man sprayed the desk and Corey slapped his arm. Corey was five-eight, maybe a hundred sixty pounds and hovered somewhere around fifty years old. The naked man, Gary Glock he was called, looked about twenty-four, was six-three and was two hundred thirty pounds easy.

"Can't you see I'm doin' somethin' here with my friend?" Corey said, putting his hands on his hips.

"Look, buddy, I'm just trying to get done so I can go home. I—"

"I'm not ya fuckin' buddy. Bitch, I'm doin' somethin' here. Be elsewhere."

Usually when Corey popped off it was harmless. Once he got out his initial volley, he lost the wind in his sails and moved onto something else. The guy had the attention span of a horsefly.

Median had tuned him out, mostly, looking for Celeste at the locker room door.

Until the kid said the wrong thing.

"Look, I don't work for you people, I just do a job."

"Whoa-whoa-whoa! What did you say? *You* people? What the hell is that supposed to mean?"

"Look, C, let the guy just finish up," Median said. "It's been a long day."

"No-no. The kid's got his big boy drawers on. Let him explain himself."

Something about Corey's tone and body language must have impressed upon Gary and he took a small step back. Another mistake. If Corey could intimidate you that made him bolder.

"I'm not asking for trouble. I apologize. *Please.*"

Asking for mercy. Strike three.

Median was about to step in between them to head off what was about to happen but Corey was too quick. His arm flashed and Gary stumbled backward. He blinked a couple times then realized he'd been hit. As pretty as he was, his face was almost hideous when he snarled and charged Corey.

He grabbed him by the lapels and lifted him, shaking him in the air as he continued moving and throwing Corey down.

Corey was smiling as he rolled over onto his side and up to one knee as Gary came on again. Median didn't see if he had anything in his hand but he thought he saw the glint of metal as Gary got closer and Corey threw another of those laser-fast blows. It landed solidly with his face but Gary

37

wasn't stung like before, although blood immediately began pouring from his face.

He went low, hammering Corey in the ribs with monster uppercuts that might have lifted the smaller man off his feet with each contact. But he stayed upright, his much smaller fists connecting with Gary's face over and over again.

Gary threw a right Corey barely got out of the way of but was off balance and not fast enough to dodge the left hook that caught him square in the jaw. He fell and Gary was on top of him before he could bounce back up. He hammered Corey with the bottoms of his fists, the smaller man's head drumming off the concrete floor.

People were shouting and standing around. Median had frozen just a moment but moved in to try to break up the fight. But it was over by the time he'd walked the three feet to reach them. Corey, face bloodied, had a handful of Gary's balls and was squeezing, the happiest Median had ever seen him.

"What now, motherfucker! 'You people' me now!"

Gary had rolled back onto his butt, half cradled over himself, feebly pulling at Corey's arm.

"Hey! Hey!" Corey said. "Look at me." The younger man looked up, tears in his eyes and his lip so badly lacerated Median could see his back teeth on one side soaking in blood. Corey struck him on the point of his chin and Gary slumped over, unconscious.

"Jesus! Corey!" Median grabbed him under the arm and rushed him over to the food service table, which was just donuts Melly Shush had brought in.

"What?" Corey said, looking like he didn't know what had just happened. Median grabbed a fistful of napkins and shook one off, twisting up a corner and shoving it up Corey's bloody nostril. He did the same with the other side all while Corey laughed, his mouth full of blood.

"You see me over there?" Kid's young enough to be my son, the cocksucker. A man and a woman Median didn't know were helping Gary Glock to his feet. The lights were still coming on behind his eyes as they led him to the locker room.

"Shit!" Median said and stuffed the rest of the napkins in Corey's hand. He ran toward the locker room door.

"Go ahead and throw that garbage out!" Corey said. "I'm done with it."

He pushed the door open and went in. Past the lockers was a communal shower area. The only people in here were the other two guys in the foursome with Celeste. One was still showering while the other had a towel wrapped around him as they talked.

Median went back the way he'd come and looked beneath the stall partitions to see if she was on the toilet. Nobody. Then he ran back to the door, holding it open long enough for the two people holding Gary between them to get through them he ran for the exit.

There was one less car in the parking lot, although a few more people had filtered out. He couldn't remember what kind of car it had been and swore under his breath.

## Chapter 8. Where are My Pants? Part I

Something jarred Median awake. For a long period he was still, trying to remember where he was. The last thing he remembered was getting sick outside the bathroom. Something told him not to call out and he listened for several long moments.

When he finally moved he panicked because something was pinning his arms to his chest. He finally struggled a hand free and felt around. He was in a bathtub, wrapped up in a shower liner like a burrito.

It took him several minutes to get out but Median finally crawled over the lip of the tub. His limbs felt heavy and weak. He needed something to eat and worse still he needed to pee. He rolled over and managed to pull himself onto the toilet.

He noted two things and had to speak out loud to process them. "Where are my pants?" He said and "What the hell?"

In fact his pants and underwear were gone but more shocking was the beer belly he suddenly had. It wasn't huge but it shouldn't have been there. Median wasn't as fit as he'd like to have been but he'd never let himself get *this* out of shape. He laughed because he kind of looked like he was preg—

"Goddammit!"

Everything returned to him as he finished going number one. He shook off and stood, reaching for ghostly pants and underwear. He half considered not flushing the toilet as a means of one-upping Mariah but in the end couldn't. Not flushing was wrong.

He washed his hands too and spied his protruding belly again in the mirror. He lifted his shirt and sure enough that was his stomach. Looked like he was about three or four months.

He had to go see his wife. She'd know what to do. But first he had to get out of this house and avoid Mariah while he did it.

He was a little foggy on what she'd said to him but he remembered it not sounding pleasant. Something to do with his baby.

Shit. *His* baby.

Was that what it was now? This morning had started like a normal day, except for the throwing up part and here he was, accepting that he was pregnant with the devil's baby.

Speaking of weird shit, though, was the head okay? It was odd that he was concerned. For all he knew several hours had passed and the head could be freezing his...*head* off in his car.

He flipped off the bathroom light and crept to the door. He turned the handle slowly and pulled, praying the door didn't squeak.

Median breathed a sigh of relief and felt terror all over again. Mariah was all over the place but mostly a big chunk of her was a few feet away on the floor.

He squished across the carpet toward the door, not sure if whoever had done that was still here. Something tapped him on the shoulder and he screamed before realizing it was just a piece of her skull that had dropped from the ceiling.

Median covered his mouth with one hand, having enough bravery to explore the kitchen and finding his pants in the garbage. He hopped to the door, pulling off his socks as he went, not knowing what had happened to his shoes and not caring to find out.

This would have been the moment when the killer had barred the door somehow, catching Median in his (or her—come on, people) trap but as he unlocked the door and opened it he looked around one last time, seeing the house was in shambles but no one wielding an axe.

He was relieved to see his car still parked where he'd left it but figured this was the second most likely place the killer would spring *her or his* trap. He looked up and down the street and didn't feel like he was being watched.

Then he noticed his passenger window had been smashed. And the head and the box it had been in were gone.

"Dammit," he said.

## Chapter 9. - Pete Parvin

Some people believe I lost my lid but they don't know the truth. Sure, it takes a sucker to believe his own tale but I know the lie. *I* know I was on a TV show in the 80s. Solid number three slot for two seasons then nada.

Canceled.

Acting had been all I ever had. Every relationship fell by the wayside in pursuit of a dream. And in the space of those two years I had everything. TV Guide, that other TV magazine that comes in newspapers nobody read because they had TV Guide already. Even got a Grammy nom for Best Second Unit Director. And then. . .

Canceled.

I'd left my wife back home to take this role, knowing I could win her back. But when my whole life got pulled from underneath me I had nothing. I'd been. . .

Canceled.

Until I heard them. The victims who still needed Hammercock. They spoke to me, they still cried out for justice as only he had handed it out. They cried out for *me*. The show was gone but there was an all-time ratings high inside me. I had to carry on whether the cameras were there or not. I had to make my own script.

And I did. I still caught the bad guys. The small-time hustlers, the pimps, the killers, the cheats. And the fans came *back*. People began to take notice. And eventually I made it here. On the case of all cases. Workin' for the good guys.

There's no way the show can't get a third season now. What TV exec is gonna tell the Guy Upstairs no?

I climb out the bucket, parked behind the vehicle belonging to the man of the hour. Suzanne is startin' to get itchy in her holster.

"There-there, girl," I say to her. She's good at her work but sometimes over eager. Walker

Harris is the only one we're here for. I'll kill him
like the angel wanted and bring his head as proof.

I give the front door a rap and press on the
buzzer too. It takes a minute while I hear somebody
rattling around inside. Then she comes.

The most beautiful dame a sucker ever could
lay eyes on. She has a look like anybody could
touch her but nobody could have her.

"How may I help you?" She is divine,
wrapped in a silk robe that does nothing to hide her
assets. As demure as she tries to make herself she
comes off as everything sylphidine. I recognize a
nymph when I see one. A distraction just before the
goal. But I earned these whiskers by seeing a thing
for what it is.

"You can back up," I say, drawing Suzanne
and aiming between her eyebrows and hairline.

Her eyes go wide with surprise but she's
smart enough not to scream.

"Where is he?" I ask as I invite myself
inside. I can tell by her eyes she's a wily one and
she dispenses with the pretense.

She shrugs. "He left right before you got
here."

I smile. "Is that why his car's still parked
outside?"

"He saw you coming and ducked out the
back."

I know it's a lie even though I don't know
it's a lie. "I put a tripwire just outside the back door.
Fish line, too thin to see unless it's an inch away
from your face. Considering the back half of your

44

house is still attached to the front half I'm pretty sure nobody went out that way."

"What if I told you I was lying?" she says, daring to come closer and I let her. "What if there isn't a backdoor?"

"Everybody's got a backdoor." I say.

"How do you know?" She crosses right by me and bends over, putting her hands on the mantel. "Unless you check?"

I could probably pat her down all day long and I bet she'd still be armed. This is the wrong woman to make a mistake with and if I'm not careful I might fall into the wrong hole. I approach, gun at the ready, and I'm not satisfied until I'm done with a rigorous frisking.

"Lead the way." I let her by and watch her close as she walks down the hall. She could hook a man like a fish with her curves alone and I don't stand a chance in Hades if she takes off even a stitch of clothing. "Hold on," I tell her and open the linen closet. I grab a fistful of towels and toss them at her. "Cover up."

She wraps a towel around her waist with a coy smile and I have her put one across her shoulders too. My heart slows to the speed of a machine gun and I motion for her to go on.

"Take the covers off the bed," I say. She pulls them off and I motion for her to face the wall. I peek under the bed and there's no boogey man and no Walker Harris either.

"Look, I'll make a deal with you," I say to her. "You tell me where he is now and you get to walk out of here in fewer than two pieces."

"No." She laughs and even that is like a cherub. "This is my house." She folds her arms beneath a cleavage that's like two walls of flesh trying to climb over one another. "How about I make you a deal?"

"How about I say I'm intrigued?"

She nods to the bed. "Pull down your pants and get on the bed and I'll give you a blow job so good your head'll cave in."

I take a proper pause to consider life-ending pleasure. This kind of offer comes along on twice in a lifetime. Once if you take the first offer.

I take a big step forward. "I'll pass."

"You sure? I wouldn't want you to leave empty-handed."

"Maybe you missed it but I am holding a pretty big gun."

She grabs me by the brain and says, "Probably bigger than a thimble. Slightly shorter than a rolling pen."

"You flatter me, ma'am," I say. For three seconds I'm tempted, but the angel comes back to mind. Nothing she could offer me could compare to what I might get with him. "I got a better offer and I don't want to screw it up."

"You could always take both. One last offer." She drops the towel and the robe before laying back on the bed, putting her arms above her head and putting her legs up like she means every word she says. "I won't tell."

Temptation rears its mushroom-shaped head again as I realize I'm someplace south of heaven. "No. I bet you wouldn't. But it's a risk I can't take, see? Now get yourself decent or I'll shoot you." I speak through numb lips, every inch of me wants to be inside of her.

"I've never had a man turn me down before," she says.

"Well, don't think of it as being turned down. Think of it as me turning myself up."

"What?"

"Never mind with the fun and games. I got business to tend."

She gets up and fixes me with a glare as evil as Medusa on a bad hair day. Then she pops me one right on the kisser. Her lips are like two feathers lifting me right off my feet. I pull her away, our mouths like magnets.

"There's nothing for you in there, see? Quit digging around and let's get this thing done."

"Wait," she says. "Let me try one more time. Call it a professional courtesy."

I sigh like a sprung tire and nod. She stands on her tippy toes and gives it to me. Gives it to me like I've never gotten it before. I could yodel with her tongue she goes so deep. She's got to be tasting last Tuesday's breakfast. She goes on longer than my last dental hygiene appointment before we break.

She stares at me like she's looking for a review.

"Well?"

"What can I tell you, sweetheart? I'll give you four out of five stars but it still isn't enough. Give it up while they giving is still good."

"You know many men would give their fortunes to be with me. I've had kings fall to their knees before me."

"I wouldn't have doubted it twenty years ago. But a guy like me wouldn't have a down payment. And the only crown I've ever had is this bowler on top of my dome." I pinch the brim of my hat and give her a wave with the barrel of my gun.

Then she tries to run. I expected her to try at some point but she still catches me by surprise. I hadn't intended on having a scrape with her but then again she's hiding him and therefore is just as bad.

I take aim as she turns out of the bedroom, lining up right where I estimate her head will be. One shot through the wall and then the silence after the roar.

When I step out of the bedroom I see where I hit. The top half of her head is gone, or more accurately decorating the walls ceiling and carpet. Maybe my bullet went through a stud and got slowed down just enough to paint this particular masterpiece.

"No means no, doll," I said to the still twitching body on the floor.

Partial decapitation is hard on a bladder so I step into the bathroom. I'm so close I can almost touch him. I finish my business and wash my hands before searching the house myself. I figure Walker Harris isn't here, but find his weight in rubber toys.

Before I can search another room I hear a siren. Someone must have reported the gunshot so I have to get out now. I peek out the front window to see a pair of cherries as the fuzz parks across the street.

I head for the back of the house and dammit if she hadn't lied. There is no back door. I get a window open partly but years of painting over and over again makes it stick before it's open enough to get my hand through.

I probably have another minute before a knock on the door and this little house doesn't have any place to hide. I go back to the front window and see the cop wandering around like he's lost. I go to the kitchen and notice a door I hadn't seen before. I almost pass it by anyway, thinking it's a basement and a house this old probly doesn't have an egress window.

## Interlude 1. November 4th, 1860, Cannonade Plantation

This motherfucker.

I'd kill 'im if I could. I need him like I need another hole in my black ass. Escaping the plantation was all but forgot after the white man came. That little nigga was the bell of the ball after then with Ma'am Davies movin' him in the house and a' course his mama came too. Shanti couldn't just live in the house proper-like, though. Ma'am Davies sold one of them high yellow girls on account she didn't want too many negroes walkin' around. So Shanti picked up her duties.

But she was a rough one.

The baby, Alfred she was calling him, was her third, so she knew how to work around havin' a whole baby strapped to her. But Alfred wasn't allowed to cry. Or when he cried that made trouble for the rest of us.

I suppose I need to fill in a little more detail. I was moved into the house which you might think was a good thing at first, considerin' I was closer to Isis.

That old nigga Benton was finally too old to butler so he got to sit around and be boss over the rest of us. Nobody was gon' buy his ole ass and he was just as hard as Ma'am Davies. The rumor was either he was fuckin' her or she had had his pecker cut off when he was young so he could never spoil her or any of her girls. I wished for the former and prayed for the latter.

Benton had a walking stick. He was as skinny and as straight as sugar cane but you couldn't catch him without that goddamn stick and anytime Alfred cried he was libel to strike the first nigga he saw and then find out where the baby was.

My job was his old job and also followin' behind Shanti. She couldn't stop her work, rough as she was, which meant Alfred got jostled same as he wouldda been in the field. 'Ceptin' nobody care out there.

Benton showed me how to do his work. He didn't dust but he made sure the girls did it right. He didn't clean dishes or do the wash but he made sure dishes were put away and wash was folded. He didn't cook but dammit if he wasn't right next to cookie stickin' a spoon into make sure it was salted just the way Ma'am Davies likes. The joke was he knew exactly how much on account she liked her food as salty as her asshole.

I had to know how she liked her food. Heavy on salt always and butter enough to grease a man from head to toe.

If I asked a question he hit me with that stick. If I didn't catch a spot of dust he hit me with that stick. If Ma'am Davies asked for salt he hit me with that stick.

Even worse was me having to dress like him. Benton was always in a tie and vest. I had to grow out my hair and comb it like him greased back and parted down the middle.

In truth his job did come with some perks. I ate good and I had a nice enough bed in the cottage he lived in. I don't know if Benton actually slept, though. I'd hear him roamin' about at all times a' night. The cottage only had two rooms and I was surprised he actually gave me the bedroom.

"No need in it goin' ta waste," he'd said. "I ain't so much as been able to do more than sit in twenty years."

He punished one of the girls in front of me. Taffeta, I think her name was. He said she hadn't polished up the silverware good enough and dragged her out back o' the house. He made her strip down to her under things and whipped her with that stick 'til she was sobbin' and had red welts all down her back. I'd seen to the silverware and it hadn't just looked fine to me it had been fine. I think ole Benton beat Taffeta for me to see how it was done.

"Don't trust none of 'em, y'hear?" He said. "A nigga will get one over on you 'lessen you keep an eye on 'im. Sometimes two eyes. That go special for them yella ones."

He made me hit Taffeta too. I hadn't been nothin' but nice to her but she wouldn't look at me no more after that.

I did get used to his job. I'd thought field work was hard but my hands grew calluses, my feet ached something constant, and all that extra food? I still had to cinch my pants. And it seemed like I was just hittin' my stride when he passed. Benton coughed a whole lot and I'd seen the blood on his kerchief once but he always showed me away when I asked after him.

I remember I had retired for the night and was just comin' in the cottage when I saw a doctor was visitin' with him.

"It ain't gon' be much longer. Maybe he'll last through the night." Galvin Cooper, one a' Ma'am Davies nephews was with them. Galvin was all right so far as I'd experienced with him. As all right as you could expect anybody white to be.

The two men shook hands and the doctor parted, rufflin' my nappy head as he left.

"Get over here, Bighead," Galvin said. He knew I could read and had taken to callin' me that as a joke. "Looks like old Benton is gettin' ready to go to that big cotton field in the sky."

I looked at him and it was the only time I'd ever felt pity for him. I'd seen Benton just that mornin' and aside from a little bit of coughin' he'd seemed all right to me. Benton was about six-three and a good one hundred eighty pounds but his arms and legs were thin as matchsticks.

"I need to get out this bed," he said between coughs. "I cain't be layin' down like this."

"Don't you worry none, old timer," Galvin said. "You just rest." Benton didn't really seem like he was hearing anything at all and every time he tried to get up, Galvin eased him back down.

"See him through the night," he said to me. "Give him this when he needs it." He handed me a little vial filled with what looked like milk. "When he's done come to the house. Tell Tilly. The girls'll wash 'im and we'll bury him before supper."

When I was alone with the old man I made myself a meal of some beans and biscuits. I couldn't eat by him, the smell of illness was so strong on him.

He'd stopped tryin' to get out of bed, not because he was settlin' down but because his strength was failin' him. I came to check on him 'round eleven o'clock and saw him holdin' his stomach, 'least that's what it looked like.

"Yessir! Yessir!" he said. "We be sho to take *good* care of this here child." He had the most unnatural smile on his face, like he was sick and happy at the same time. Kinda like Ma'am Davies had had when the white man had come.

But Benton had never held Alfred. 'Least as far as I'd seen. In fact whenever I'd been in the same room as Alfred Benton had been nowhere to be found. So what baby was this was the ole man thinkin' he was holdin'?

"Mr. Benton, sir?" I said, touchin' him on the shoulder. He just went on cradlin' that fake baby and smilin' like he knew the devil was behind him, ignorin' me as I kept callin' him. He seemed like he was already gone and I was just talkin' to a...a echo.

"Hey you ole stankin' fuck." I punched him in the arm—not too hard, mind you but it was enough to get his attention. He kept on cradlin' that baby but the smile left his face and them rheumy eyes focused and turned on me. I can't say he recognized me but he knew I was there.

"Who baby is that?" I asked and pointed at his arms.

"This here *my* baby." I hadn't thought that ole Benton couldda had a child and while I was chewin' on that thought he kept on. "This *all* our baby. We gon' keep Adolph safe."

*Adolph?* I thought. *Who the hell is Adolph?*

On the off-chance 'Adolph' had been his boy I guessed maybe he'd been born fifty years ago or however long ago a woman mighta been willin' to let Benton put his thing in her. But he'd also said he was 'all our baby'. I shouldn't have had any idea what that meant but I did. Alfred had become 'all our baby'.

Had the white man come to Cannonade before? I had no idea how old he was but Ma'am Davies was at least fifty and Benton had grew up with Moses.

"What the hell happened to Adolph?" I asked.

"Nothin'!" Benton said, that smile comin' back on his face. "He right here."

I had an idea. "You must think I'mma fool same as you. You want me to tell *him*?"

"No-no. Ain't no need for that. I—" Benton started lookin' around. "He here! Oh, god. Reg, get everybody to the root cellar. Ma'am Davies, I'm sorry, I don't know what happened. Sissy! Oh, Sissy. Let me just put my arms around you this once. If we gon' die I want to do it with my love."

"Shiiiiiiiit," I said, not meanin' to speak. Nobody ever Ma'am Davies' by her first name so far as I ever heard.

"Where the baby?" Benton said, ignorin' me. "Reggie, no, don't go back out there. Leave him! No, Sissy, that's my brother! No-no-no!"

Benton screamed like I ain't never heard no man or animal scream in my life. I about fell over like I'd been slapped by a dog as he bucked and kicked in bed. For just a moment as I was half laid on the floor I thought I saw somethin' hangin' over his bed. A face—moon white—with black scoops for eyes and a smile like...like a woman's...a woman's. . .

It was horrible to see and just as bad to recall. It wasn't real no how.

Maybe it was a trick of the light, the moon behind the clouds. It wasn't until later that I realized the window over Benton's bed was on the opposite side of where the moon shined.

"Benton?" I said. "Sir?" I rose and approached him slow. His body was still propped up, back bowed inward, his belly pointed at the ceilin'. I took the covers off him and saw only the top of his head and the heels of his feet were on the bed. Now I done seen a few folk die before but never this. And Benton was for sho dead.

I held a mirror up to his mouth anyway to make sure. His mouth was all foamed up like a rabid dog and his eyes rolled up in his head. I put my hand on his middle to try to ease him back down and he collapsed.

I screamed myself when the last breath came outta him. It was like he was tryin' to tell me somethin' even after he'd died.

"Miiiiiiiiiloooooooo," it sounded like he'd said. Milo was my given name but almost everybody called me Man-man. Well, everybody in the field. In the house I was Milo to everybody 'cept Benton. He always called me 'boy'.

"Mr. Benton, sir? You 'live?" I stood by him a long time before I could move. He didn't say another word, though. He was really dead. But he'd told me all I needed to know.

I had to protect Alfred no matter what.

## Chapter 10. - Joe

Whoever had taken the head had left a note. Median figured getting off this street as soon as possible was in his best interest. He needed a place to hide out and knew just the place.

He opened the note while he was stopped at a red light.

56

I HAVE YOUR SECRET, it read. IF YOU
WANT TO KEEP THE CAT IN THE BAG MEET
ME AT MIDNIGHT AT THE RIVER.

Keep the cat in the bag? What in the hell did
that mean? Median wasn't even sure if he needed
the head. Sure, it had told him things that had turned
out to be true but how much more use could he get
out of it? He didn't owe it anything, did he? It was
dead for crying out loud.

He took his cell out of the glove box and
turned it back on. He had several more messages
from Walt Wimmer that he deleted without
listening to and one more from Joe.

Shit. Joe.

"Hey, you didn't take anything out of the
fridge, did you?" he was asking in his message. "I
had a…cake…for a birthday party. I really need to
get that back as soon as possible. If you have it, that
is. Just call me back." Median deleted the message.
He didn't have time to ponder about Joe and his
'cake'.

Then his phone rang. It was Joe. Median
tried to hit ignore and accidentally answered.

"I'm right behind you," Joe said. "Pull
over."

Median looked in his rearview mirror and
saw his roommate driving that big ass truck of his.
He could try to out maneuver him and lose him in a
series of left and right turns down side streets and
alleyways, speeding and slowing strategically, and
doing that one move when you stepped on the gas
and the brake at the same time and yanked the
wheel as hard as possible to one side.

But Median had a four-cylinder Chevy Cruze and Joe's Silverado looked like it could eat his car. Maybe he could figure this out a different way. He pulled into a shopping plaza that appeared to only have a Subway and a dry-cleaners as tenants and carefully parked in one of the many available spots. Joe parked next to him across three spots.

He left the engine running as he hopped down and Median climbed out of his car.

"So...you get my message?" Joe asked.

"Yeah. I just listened to it."

"So? Where's my cake?"

Median didn't feel like playing this game. Besides, he was hungry.

"You want something to eat? I could go for a lightly toasted steak and cheese."

"No, man. I am not hungry. I just need my cake. I need to get to my party."

Median sighed. He locked his doors and headed for Subway.

"Hey!" Joe jogged to catch up with him then lagged back a couple steps. "What the hell happened to you?"

"What?" Median looked at Joe and saw his eyes trained on his stomach. He looked down and saw he had what looked like a bowling ball in his shirt. His back had been hurting since Mariah's house and now he could see why. "Nothing," he said to Joe. "I'm just...retaining water."

Joe opened the door and let Median go in first. Median could feel his eyes on him the whole time they were in line and wound up getting a meatball sub on white bread. Median got his steak and cheese, Baked Lays, two oatmeal raisin cookies and a diet Coke.

"You know he's going to get you," the young woman who rang up his order said. She held up her hands so he could see the backs of her fingers. 'H-A-I-L' the fingers of her right hand read and 'S-A-T-N' on the other. "Would you like your receipt?"

Joe and Median sat together and Joe blessed his food before he started eating.

"The cake," he finally said after finishing about half of his footlong.

"C'mon, we both know that wasn't a cake any more than I'm just retaining water."

"What do you mean? Did you *eat*…my cake?"

"I saw what's inside the box, Joe. Hang on." Median had drained his diet Coke and got up for a refill.

"Only one refill per customer, please," Jessi said from the other side of the counter.

Median sat back down to Joe nervously tapping the table with his fingertips.

"It isn't mine. I can explain."

"I *would* like an explanation," Median said. "But let me tell you something first. I'm pregnant."

"*What?*"

"You heard me." Median leaned forward. "Keep your voice down."

The confession was ridiculous enough to make Joe laugh even though he was clearly unnerved. "It isn't mine."

"No. It's the devil's."

"The devil? Median, what the hell are you talking about?"

"I was…working yesterday. I felt a pain…in my ass…and I guess after that I was pregnant."

"I thought I was about to have to explain away something weird. You already beat me to the punch."

"What I really need to know right now is should I be afraid of you?"

"Me? No!" Joe looked around then leaned forward to whisper. "The…*head* isn't what you think it is. I found that."

"Right."

"I'm serious. Look, other than that one time I told you about, I ain't never killed anybody before."

"Then why did you bring it home?"

"I'm working on an…art project."

"Art project?"

"You ever see the movie *Pieces*?"

"I don't think so."

"Spanish movie about a Boston serial killer. The details aren't so much important. Somebody tells me where the bodies are and what parts to take."

"So you're working with a serial killer?"

"What? No! He—or she—tells me where the bodies are. I've never met the killer."

"And you're totally okay with that?"

"No." Joe shook his head. "I don't have a choice. And the killer has assured me all the people he's killed were bad people."

That rang a little true for Median. The head had told him it hadn't lead a good life.

"So what's the point of collecting these parts? And why haven't you gone to the police?"

"I can give you one answer to both. He's—*or she's*—on a mission. Once I've finished, the murders will stop. And he—*or she*—removes the bodies after I've taken whatever part. They aren't even reported as missing. It's like they've been erased."

"Do you have any idea who it is? Or who the people are he—*or she*—is killing?"

"No. I wouldn't be doing any of this if he—*or she*—hadn't clearly communicated to me that I had no choice."

"What do you mean?"

Joe took out his cell and opened his photos. He scrolled through several pictures then pushed the phone over to Median.

"The last guy he had collecting parts decided he didn't want to do it anymore. He—or she—said that would happen to me if I halted the work."

It took a moment for Median to recognize the bloody pieces made one person. He assembled them in his head like a puzzle.

"That was a man?" he asked, munching chips.

Joe nodded. "And he—or she—snuck into the apartment and took a picture of me sleeping with a knife to my throat."

Median sat back, chewing his last bite of sub. "What are you going to do?"

"Well first I'm going to get that head back from you."

"I don't have it," Median said. "Somebody stole it out of my car."

"Why did you even take it? Who took it?"

"Not sure but he left me this." Median gave the note and to Joe.

"Is this for real?"

"I guess. He took the box and left that in my passenger seat."

"Well let's get down there."

"Why? We have like five hours to go. I'm not so sure that's a good idea anyway. I think he wants to get me."

"Okay. Okay. Here's what we do. Whoever this is probably doesn't know about me, right? I go down there early and kind of hang in the background and when this guy shows up I bop him on the head and get my head back."

Median slowly rose from his seat. "I gotta pee." His stomach looked even bigger.

"Whoa," Joe said. "You didn't have that this morning. Are you for real that you're pregnant by the *devil*? I mean, how do you know?"

Median didn't want to tell him how he knew so he just shrugged.

"And how are you supposed to give birth?"

Median shrugged again.

After he came out of the restroom he grabbed his cup for another refill.

"Just one per customer!" Jessi said again. Joe poured the rest of his drink out and refilled with diet Coke. Then he handed it to Median. The teen stared holes into Joe, obviously not liking this particular loophole.

"So where are we going until tonight?"

"We?" Median said.

"Yeah. You don't seriously think you can go anywhere in your car, do you? He probably has it bugged."

Median hadn't thought of that.

"I guess you're driving me to my wife's place."

## Chapter 11. - Mrs. Harris

"Come in!" Mary said. It had begun raining on the way over and Median and Joe hustled inside. "You two want something hot to drink to warm you up?"

"Tea would be amazing," Joe said.

"None for me—on second thought, vodka cranberry?" Median said.

She went into the kitchen and Joe looked at him.

"You should tell her."

"I know I *should* but *how*?"

Joe gave him a look. "Just tell her. You want me to do it? 'Cause I'll do it."

"No." Median looked at Joe. "No."

"Tell me what?" Mary asked, coming out of the kitchen. Median scratched his head then let his hand trail down to the bottom of his shirt. He lifted it.

"Median, why does your stomach look like you ate a bowling ball?"

"I'm pregnant."

She came over and hugged him. After a few seconds he tried to pull back and she locked onto him tighter. Finally, she pulled away but she kept her hands on his shoulders.

"Are you okay?"

"Uh, yeah," Median said and suddenly began crying. "No!" She pulled him in for another hug and he let it all out.

"There-there," Mary said. She let him go until his sobs subsided.

"I don't know why this is happening to me," Median said.

"Come here, sit down." She guided him over to the couch and sat with him. "Joe, could you take care of drinks? Teabags are on top of the refrigerator."

Joe left as she stroked Median's head, holding his hand in her lap.

"I'm pregnant with the devil's baby."

"May I?" Mary held her hand above his tummy.

"I guess." Median didn't really want her to but she'd always wanted to have a baby. Considering they were still married technically she was this baby's mother. She put her hand on him and he felt something move. It was uncomfortable as hell and surprising.

"Whoa!" she said. "That's a big boy."

"How do you know it's a boy?"

"You're carrying low."

"What the hell is he doing?"

"Aw, he's saying hello." She moved her hand over and tapped the side of his stomach. "See?"

Median looked at his protruding belly and dammit if it didn't look like a three-fingered hand was pressing against it from the inside.

"The *fuck*?"

"What's wrong?"

"It has three fingers!"

"Oh, pish. You can't tell that through your stomach. Even if it does only have three fingers, wouldn't you still love him?"

Median looked at her in disgust. "*Love*? I want it out of me."

Mary made a face. "You don't want to keep it?"

"Mary." He sat up. "I'm a guy. Guys aren't supposed to be pregnant. Especially by the devil. Can you help me or no?"

"Tea's here!" Joe came back with two steaming cups in one hand and a gin glass he handed Median. Median pounded the vodka cranberry back.

"I support you, Walker. But I don't agree with what you want to do. That's a life."

"I didn't ask for this. And even if I could have chosen to get pregnant I wouldn't pick satan to be the father."

She nodded. "I know a place."

## Chapter 12. A Bag of Nuts

It was a nondescript place in a shopping plaza on the east side. The sign above the entrance read 'Family Health'. Joe had driven and had elected to stay in the truck. Median had put on a heavy coat to cover himself. His ankles and his back were killing him. They entered, not looking at anyone in the waiting room, and headed right for the receptionist's desk. Mary took the paperwork from a fiftyish-looking woman with a big head of curly red hair and batwing glasses while Median found two seats next to a wall-mounted television.

"I'll fill out everything," she said, sitting with him. "Just sign."

He nodded, his stomach groaning, although he didn't know if it was upset or he was hungry again.

"You ever been in here before?" He looked around. There were about a dozen people here, most of them looked younger than twenty-five. A girl with long red braids who couldn't have been older than sixteen sat by herself, clutching a white teddy bear. There was a man and woman sitting in the seats across from them who had equally blank expressions and tightly holding hands. There was also a heavyset woman with three children hovering around her who ranged from two to four years old.

A woman in scrubs opened a door and called a name. The sixteen year old stood while still looking at the floor. She walked silently past the woman holding the door open and disappeared inside.

"She's just a kid." Median shook his head.

Mary didn't say anything. She just smiled at him and grabbed his hand and gave it a squeeze. For the next hour people came in and out, nobody making eye contact.

"Walker Harris," the woman said at the door. He stood.

Mary didn't.

"You gotta come with me!" he whispered.

"No, I don't, Walker."

"But they can see I'm not a...y'know." He gestured to his genitalia.

She laughed. "Don't you think they're going to figure that out at some point? For all they know you're transgender."

"I. . ." He hadn't thought about that.

"Walker Harris," the woman said again.

"Hurry up." Median hustled past the woman. She led him down a long hallway, passing several closed doors.

"Number five," she said. The woman sounded tired. She let Median go in first and closed the door behind them. She took his blood pressure and temperature and made some notes on a clipboard.

"Please take off your clothes and put on this gown. Leave it open in the back. You can leave your socks on or take them off but put your feet in the stirrups. Dr. Rick will be with you in a few."

She left without saying anything more and Median realized he hadn't gotten her name. He took his time taking off his clothes. Median was used to being naked in front of other people but this was definitely different. How was this going to work?

And Dr. Rick? What kind of name was that for a doctor? Was that a first or last name?

He had a sudden vision of a middle-aged white guy with a deeply receded hairline and a ponytail coming in in a lab coat with the sleeves rolled up.

"Let him come," Median said. "Good old Dr. Rick." He found his mind wandering as he sat back and put his feet up. Would the doctor shake his hand? How would they introduce themselves to one another?

Of all the places he could have been right now, Median let his mind wander to how he had gotten here. He thought about the circumstances beyond his control that resulted in him being in this situation.

Balls. It had all happened because of balls.

Obviously, the first pair at fault would be his father's. He and his brother hadn't been lucky enough for their dear old dad to have abandoned them after conceiving Jerry. Their old man had stuck around long enough to screw them up. He had never laid a hand on either of them or their mother but his torture had run so much deeper than anything physical could have.

He had tortured their dog and left it barely hanging onto life and encouraged median to put it out of its misery. He had also forced their mother to participate in three-way sex with men and women and Median's introduction to sex had been him walking in on his father fucking the skinniest woman he'd ever seen. It was no wonder he'd turned to porn eventually.

But the second pair of balls to let him down we're his own. He had fallen in love with Mary the day he had met her and had pledged his soul to her. She'd told him how much she wanted to have children before they were married and after failing to get pregnant for two years they had gone to a fertility specialist and found out the problem was with him. He had tried so hard to keep his marriage together but immediately she began to pull away. He knew she loved him and always would but he knew he could never be the father of the children she needed.

And the last pair of balls belonged to this devil guy. Satan, Beelzebub, Stitch—whatever the hell he called himself—his nuts were the biggest pain in his ass. Median never asked for this. Until this morning he would have said he didn't believe in a devil but now, nearly due to give birth and lacking the proper number of X chromosomes, he couldn't deny the existence of *something* supernatural at play. Who was this guy and who had given him access to Median's body?

"Hi, Dr. Rick. My name is Walker Harris and I'm actually a guy so don't freak out when you look down there and see a penis," he said out loud. "Why no, this isn't some sort of joke. I'm pregnant with the devil's baby. Not *the* devil, but one of them as hell is apparently filled with a multitude of devils. Yeah, it doesn't make much sense to me, either but maybe after we get all this business sorted you and I can have a sit down and talk all about it."

There was a knock on the door.

It felt like the room had suddenly risen twenty degrees in temperature.

"Mr. Harris," the doctor said as he entered the room, holding a chart and what looked like a Ziplock bag of cashews. "How are you today?" 'Sun Goddess' by Earth, Wind, and Fire began playing overhead.

"Good, I suppose." Median looked over the man as he shut the door behind himself and dammit if he didn't look almost exactly like he'd pictured. A little thinner on top but his hair was onyx and pulled into a neat pony that almost looked like the business end of a paintbrush. He had on rimless glasses, had a nose piercing, and a brush of a blondish-red vandyke.

He didn't offer to shake hands or even make eye contact with Median, instead sitting the chart and the sack down and washing his hands carefully in the sink.

Median wondered if there was supposed to be a nurse or someone else in the room as Dr. Rick shook the excess water from his hands and then dabbed them dry with a paper towel. He came over and put a hand on Median's belly and smiled. Median thought he looked a little like that Swedish actor who looked like Bruce Willis.

"Let's see what we have here." He smiled wide and stepped around and pulled the little wheeled chair up and sat, getting a good look between Median's legs.

"So you want this outta you?" he asked. Median noticed he hadn't strapped on a pair of gloves.

What kind of question—

"Hell yes!" Median shouted, realizing something just as he spoke. "You called me Mr. Harris. You know I'm a guy?"

"Well if I didn't know before, the ding-dong staring at me is a clue. A big clue I might add."

He gave the head of Median's penis a tap and a chill ran up his thighs. Median tried to pull his feet out of the stirrups but they were stuck.

"Wait a minute—who are you?"

"Who do you think I am?" Dr. Rick slowly stood. He was still snacking, the plastic sack of cashews in hand somehow. He saw Median's eyes on the nuts. "Want one?"

Median had an aversion to all nuts. He was already freaked out by being in this place and then to have a doctor trying to feed him, let alone something he thought was disgusting, let alone the doctor himself was eating. Everything about what was happening right now was wrong.

Aaaaaand if he was being totally honest a part of him *wanted* to keep this baby.

*His* baby.

Median was about to speak up again when he realized several things at once.

Dr. Rick had referred to him as 'mister' when he came in. *Before* peaking under the gown.

Median tried pulling his feet out of the stirrups again but the clamps felt even tighter.

"Are you…are you the devil?"

Dr. Rick smiled.

"Are you the one who got me pregnant?"

The doctor leaned against the wall and popped another nut in his mouth. Median had caught a glimpse and that had been no cashew. It had looked like a veiny white grape.

Dr. Rick must have seen him looking. "You sure you don't want one?" He held the bag open so Median could see inside and he wished he hadn't looked. Median hadn't seen an actual testicle before but he was reasonably certain he was looking at a whole cluster of them.

His vision of the doctor blurred and he had a long moment of something akin to motion sickness like the doctor was far away and up close at the same time. He eventually recognized he was seeing two differing images of the same figure. Through one eye he saw the middle-aged, balding-yet-ponytailed, red-gold vandyked hippy and through the other he saw a crimson-skinned, goat-legged, snake-eyed figure with studded horns wreathed around his head.

"No," Median said, voice barely reaching his ears.

The Dr. Rick devil sat the sack on the counter by the sink and dusted his hands.

"All right, let's get this started."

"What are you going to do?" Median asked.

"Exactly what you came here for. I'm going to take that thing right out of you." He mumbled something Median couldn't hear.

"What was that?"

"Huh? Oh. I'm going to take that baby right on out." Then he mumbled something again.

72

"I heard the taking the baby out part. What are you going to do after?"

Dr. Rick rolled his eyes and sighed. "I'm going to take the baby out and then put the right one in."

"What do you mean 'put the right one in'?"

"That—" he pointed to Median's middle— "is not my seed. I don't know whose it is."

"What do you mean, not yours? You're the whole reason I'm here."

"Yeah, no. You're pregnant because of me but you aren't pregnant with *my* seed."

"The fuck you talkin'?"

"I'm not shitting. That hottie Mariah Moore was supposed to carry my seed. But there was a series of calamities, one of which being you getting pregnant instead of her and the other—"

"Somebody's else's seed—" Median gestured to his belly.

"Bingo. So I'm going to correct the error. Personally. No more middlemen."

"But if it's a mistake why not just impregnate Mariah? She already said she wanted to carry your baby."

"Too late now." Dr. Rick shook his head. "Everybody knows you're pregnant with my seed. I got a name to protect."

"But you just said I'm not pregnant with your...*seed*."

Rick shook his head. "M'man, perception is everything in my business." He cocked his head to the side and stepped closer, taking Median's wrist between his thumb and index. "Your pulse is up. Are you afraid?"

"*Yes.* You're the fucking devil!"

"But I'm not going to kill you. I *owe* you. I don't even want your soul."

Median just stared at him.

"Well?"

"Well what?"

"What do you want?"

"What do you mean, what do I want? You mean like anything?"

"Yes. I mean within reason. Fifty thousand dollars. The girl of your dreams for a night. Or the guy—I don't judge."

"I don't know. Could you answer something for me? I mean, in addition to the wish or whatever?"

"You know what? Usually, I would tie you up in a pretzel for asking something like that. But shoot—what do you want to know? I am hemi-omnipotent."

"Does my father have a love-child?"

Rick choked off a laugh and covered his mouth. "I'm sorry. I'm sorry. I don't mean to laugh. It's just that I haven't heard that term in so long."

"Well, do I?"

"You mean Carmen? How'd you find out? Your mother made him swear to never tell you."

"Really lucky guess."

Rick stared at him for a long moment then grinned. "Playing 'em close to the chest. I respect that. So what do you want for your actual wish?"

"I want the girl. The woman." Rick came close enough he could have rubbed noses with him. Both images consolidated into an amalgamation that was simultaneously more human than the doctor and more sinister than the demon.

"The girl. Of course. There's always 'a girl'. What's her name?"

"Celeste. I don't know her last name."

Rick smiled. "Aladdin rules apply, y'know."

"Aladdin rules?"

"Like the genie in Aladdin. I can't make her fall in love with you or bring her back from the dead. Well, I actually can but it's kinda gross. I guess I can technically subvert human will and make her appear to be in love with you or I can just flat out make her your sex slave—"

"That's okay. I just want to see her again. Is she…still alive?"

"…Yes." Dr. Rick put his hands together and put his index fingers to his mouth. "You're making all kinds of mistakes right now that normally I'd love to take advantage of but because you're my bro I wanna put you up on game."

Median stared at him blankly.

"For the sake of this conversation I'm the devil, right? What do I do?"

"Uh, lie?"

"Yes, but more specific to a situation like this I would grant your wish but in some twisted way you weren't anticipating. Sometimes that's not my fault. It's like Plinko on 'Price is Right'. You put your chip down in a certain spot and you want to win the $10,000 but there are all kinds of factors you aren't seeing. The boys in the back office get up to tricks. So I need you to say it in a very *specific* way."

"Okay."

"First off, are you cool if she's married?"

"I, uh. . ."

"Doesn't matter. Doesn't matter. She isn't married. How about if she's got kids and weighs three hundred pounds?"

"Well, I mean. . ."

"I'm fuckin' with you. She's still a hundred twenty-three pounds. That's actually two pounds less than the last time you saw her. She just got over the flu last week. What if she's been maimed or otherwise disfigured?"

"Oh my god. Has—"

"No-no." Rick waved him off. "She's got all her fingers and toes. No diseases. Look, I'm going to level with you. She's pretty much unchanged from the last time you saw her. She dyed her hair purple, though. Is that a deal breaker?"

"No!"

"Cool. So you just want to, what—sit down and have a conversation with her?"

"Yes. I don't want you to do anything. I just want to sit down and talk to her."

"Lunch good?"

"Yeah."

"Your treat?"

"Lunch is fine. Whatever she wants."

"You know she just started seeing a guy."

Median's stomach fell.

"I'm fuckin' around. She went on a couple dates with him. She's not going to see him again."

"How do you know that?"

"Because he's on my roster. I'll be seeing him in about eighteen hours."

"*Shit.*"

"So that's it? Just the girl to sit down with you for one meal?"

Median thought about it for a long moment. He wanted her to choose to be with him of her own free will. It just wouldn't feel right if she weren't really into it. He thought he could live with it if he could just talk to her and she turned him down.

"Just her. One meal."

"Okay. Then all we gotta do is this little thing and I'll set it up. You'll need about three or four weeks to recover and boom, you're in."

"Three or four *weeks*?" Median said.

"Yeah, but we're both getting what we want here, right?"

"What are you gonna do?"

"Come on. We don't need to go there. I mean, is it going to hurt? *Yeah.* I just thought if I approached this whole thing different than my usual we could both leave this feeling like neither one of us lost."

"I don't know. . ."

"Look, this is gonna happen. It just is, man. Let me do it the right *way* for once."

"But that's a long time. This...procedure shouldn't take that long to recover from, should it?"

"No, but two things: it's not a regular pregnancy and you're a dude."

Median stared at him.

"A woman's body is built to handle holding and nurturing a new life. What's happening with you right now is wreaking havoc. Not gonna kill you or anything like that. It's just changing you in ways that will affect you a lot more than if you were a woman."

"You said it's not a regular pregnancy. I figured that much, but what do you mean?"

Rick was suddenly standing next to him with an ultrasound machine and a tube of gel in one hand.

"Let me show you." He lifted Median's gown and smeared a generous amount of goo on his swollen belly. A moment later the ultrasound machine was on and he had the business end on Median's stomach.

They both watched on the little screen as Rick moved around the probe. Median didn't know what he was seeing.

"There's nothing in there according to the ultrasound."

"But—" Median gestured to his big belly.

"I know. It's not a regular pregnancy." He put the probe back in its holster and turned off the sonograph. He folded his arms. "So what's it gonna be? If you want something more I want you to have it."

Median thought a long moment. He'd been passing through his own life for the last few years. Nothing had had meaning for the longest time until the day he'd seen Celeste. He could have just been idealizing her but he had to believe there was something more. There wasn't anything more he could think of in the world he wanted more than just to be able to talk to her. To let her know he existed and see where things went from there.

He shook his head.

"Okay, then let's get started," the doctor said. He wheeled over a cart with a tray on it. Median noted the devil hadn't put on gloves and then he saw the tools on the tray.

They were laid out on a paper towel and while everything looked neat and prepared, he'd never seen medical instruments like these. One looked like an oversized scalpel with a hook on the underside of its blade. Next to that was a pair of what he guessed was a pair of pliers but the working ends were blunt-looking with grooves in them that made the heads look like teeth. Next to those was something that looked like it was made to pick a gigantic lock.

"Wait," Median said.

Rick looked up as if he'd only half heard.

Then somebody burst into the room.

A moment later somebody was screaming.

## Chapter 12. - Rhinestone

Joe didn't like sitting in the truck. He thought he should be inside with Mary and Median. Her explanation had made perfect sense. They would go in together like a couple. Median would go in instead of her and once they understood the situation they'd perform the procedure and the two of them would be out.

First off, Joe had to pee really bad in the first ten minutes. He thought about going in and asking to use the restroom but a single guy coming in to use the facilities would be weird. Besides, protesters were now outside and he didn't want to be bothered with them.

So he went to the CVS instead. Joe used the restroom and bought himself a bag of Better Made hot chips and a grape Faygo. He polished off the chips in his truck but had only gotten through half of the pop before he needed to pee again. He went back to the CVS and this time bothered to walk around several aisles with an expression like he was in the middle of making an important purchasing decision.

He found a package of rhinestones on a shelf and they took him back to a time when he was a teenager. The guy who cut his hair had described him as having 'Grade A' hair. At the time Joe hadn't known what that had meant but sometime later the barber had asked him to be in a hair show. He'd shaved a rudimentary car into the back of his head and had hair-glued rhinestones all over it.

Joe had bought the rhinestones on a lark. He'd had no real use for them. When he got back to his truck he opened the pack and poured them into his hand. Then he wished he hadn't opened the package so he could take them back. He almost threw them out the window but for some reason he tossed them into the passenger seat.

They fell in a pattern that made a perfect 'S'.

"Hm," Joe said.

He picked them up again, shook them around in his fist, then tossed them into the passenger seat again.

'A'.

Now that was really odd. He could get behind them falling in an 'S' pattern but 'A'? Was that even possible?

He picked them up again and tossed them.

A 'V'.

He picked them up and tossed them immediately.

'E'.

He recalled the letters.

"Save," Joe said aloud. "Save what?"

He tossed the stones again and again, getting the letters 'M-E-D'.

Alarms were going off in his head. He tossed the stones three more times, fearing what letters they would make.

"Save Median." Joe pursed his lips and looked toward the door where Mary and Median had gone in. "Oh, hell no."

He got out of his truck and stalked toward the clinic. The two protestors watched as he walked past him.

"Amen, brother!" the woman said.

He pushed his way inside and spotted Mary sitting beneath the television.

"Where is he?"

"He's already inside," she said.

Joe walked toward the door and pulled on the knob.

"Excuse me, sir!" the receptionist said. "Could I help you?"

"I'm here for my roommate. He's in danger."

"He—who?"

Joe yanked on the door a couple more times.

"Sir, please don't do that."

He was about to yell at her to get her to open the door but had a more efficient idea. He climbed over the counter and through the small receptionist's window. The woman's mouth fell open and she scooted back.

"Pam, call the police!" she said to the other woman in the room. Joe hopped down and walked out. He opened the first patient room door and saw a man in a white lab coat standing next to a woman in all blue talking to a girl in a paper gown who couldn't have been more than sixteen. They were showing her pictures of fetuses and the teen looked horrified. The three of them looked at him.

"Wrong room," Joe said. He'd taken a girlfriend to get an abortion before and that definitely didn't jibe with what he recalled.

He shut the door and went to the next. A woman who might have been fifty sat on the examining table. Joe noticed there were pictures of newborns and toddlers all over the wall.

"What kind of clinic is this?" he said as the woman stared at him. He didn't wait for her to respond and moved on to the next room.

"Sir! Sir!" A woman at the other end of the hall said. She was tall, thin, and dark-skinned, her shirt colored with a rainbow of squares and circles.

Joe kept moving, opening two more doors before she caught up with him. "You can't be in here, sir. We're calling the police."

"Fine," he said. "I'm sure the cops would be really interested in how you're trying to pressure women into not having abortions."

The woman's cheeks reddened, which surprised Joe considering her skin tone.

"Give me that." He yanked the stethoscope from around her neck. "Shame on you."

The woman, wide-eyed, turned around and fled. Joe opened the last door and saw this boss-looking older dude with a ponytail holding a weird-looking knife over Median's swollen belly. The 'doctor' had his back to him and Joe wasted no time crossing the room and putting his forearm to the man's shoulder blade and grabbing his wrist with the other hand. Before the doctor could complain Joe wrenched backward on his wrist, feeling a satisfying crunch. The knife-thing fell from the doctors hand and he screamed.

"Come on, let's go," Joe pulled Median's feet out of the stirrups and helped him up. He never considered Median a friend but right now he felt protective. The fake doctor was still screaming in pain, one arm hanging as he turned to see who had attacked him.

Median looked like he was in shock but he didn't fight. They walked to the door but Joe stopped, an idea popping into his head.

"Hey, doc," he said, turning to him. The doctor had stopped screaming and was cradling his injured arm. "Hold this." He kicked him in the balls and the man's eyes went wide as he fell to his knees.

He hustled Median down the hall and out the door.

"What are you doing?" Mary said.

"We're out of here," Joe said.

"But did they—"

"This is a fake abortion clinic. It's one of those places that pretends to be one." He spoke to everyone else in the room. "You hear that, everybody? This place is fucking fake.!"

The three of them left, almost jogging to the car.

## Chapter 13. Deal with a Devil

"Joe, what the hell did you just do?" Median finally asked.

"I just saved your ass. Like the rhinestones told me to do."

"What?" Mary and Median asked together.

"Crap, they're chasing us."

Joe cut the wheel hard, slamming Median into Mary against the passenger side door. He kept looking in the rearview mirror.

"Who's chasing us?" Median asked.

"Those people. Did you know that was a fake abortion clinic?"

"No, I've never been to that place. Mary—"

"Pull over right now." Mary put a gun to Median's temple.

"No way. Shoot him."

"What?" Mary and Median said together.

"I said no. Toss that fuckin' gun out the window. You're not shooting anybody and you know it."

Median watched as several expressions came over his wife's face. Finally, she cranked down the window and tossed the gun out.

"I'm never going to get my baby," she said.

*Damn! He could have asked for that too.*

"Mary," Median began. "Did you take me to that place on purpose?"

"I knew he would be there. Rick had already reached out to me and said you might be coming."

"You *know* him? He's the devil!"

"He's not *the* devil," Mary said.

"You know what I mean. Mary, you brought me to him."

"I know, I know. But he said he'd take care of you. That he'd give you whatever you wanted. And he'd give me a baby."

"Mary, you struck a deal with a demon and didn't tell me."

"Look, I'm sorry, okay?"

While they were talking, Joe was weaving through side streets, alleys, and parking lots.

"So what do we do now?" Median asked.

"We find a place to hunker down until the meet tonight," Joe said.

"You still want to do that? Really, Joe, is that head that important?"

"Yes. It's the most important thing in the world. We get that head back and everything else we can figure out later. What you need to figure out is why your wife sold you out to satanists."

"They're not satanists," Mary said. "Hell is full of devils. There is no satan, just a bunch of middle-management types all looking to screw each other over."

Median stared at her like he was seeing her for the first time.

"Don't look at me like that," Mary said. "I pursued every avenue to get pregnant and you know it, so yes, I also looked into making a deal with the devil. They're not actually bad people. They have a job to do—a heavenly mandate, by the way—and they do the best they can with it. You have to also remember the devil is also in hell. Nobody thinks about what it's like for them down there, just how their own souls will be tormented for all of eternity."

"You sound like you're friends with the guy," Joe said.

"I kind of am. Did you know every devil in hell has his own devil? Every one of them is being pursued by a devil who's slightly worse than him or her. Rick is trying to *change* things."

"Change things how?" Median asked.

"They all have a quota to fill and hell is already filled past capacity. It can be up to a hundred years to get processed and out of hell's waiting room. Meanwhile, heaven is less than a quarter of one-percent full. There needs to be a change in the rules for who goes where. The current system isn't sustainable."

"You really have been talking to him," Median said.

"Yes, I have. And quite frankly I think heaven is filled with elitists."

"Elitists? Elitists how?"

"Think of space as wealth. Up there in heaven they have all this room, they can spread out as much as they want. While in hell souls are jam-packed. In heaven it's determined who goes where and how much room both places have. They intentionally made the rules so heaven is near impossible to get into and then didn't provide adequate spacing for everyone in hell. And there's no parole. How fair is that?"

"I think I get your point," Joe said. "So this Rick guy is one of these devils. He's only following the rules as they are written and when he cheats is only because he has to?"

"*Yes.* That's why when he makes deals with people he doesn't make taking their souls a part of the bargain. He's got more than he can handle already. He makes deals to get something he can actually use."

"Like having a baby." Median looked into Mary's eyes.

"Like having a baby," she said. "I'm sorry, Walker."

Considering he knew how much his wife had always wanted to have her own child his anger dissipated. He grabbed her hand and gave it a squeeze.

"But how does him having a baby with me help him? I mean doesn't he have a bunch of kids in hell already?"

"He wants something free from hell. Something not a part of the 'rat race' as he calls it. Walker, he's not going to stop until he gets his baby."

"Well if he does what it looked like he was about to do there won't be a Median left when he's done. That Rick devil guy was about to gut him."

"And he did say it would be at least three weeks for me to recuperate."

"Hang on, I'm gonna pull over here." Joe pulled into the parking lot of another plaza and went behind the building. There was a heavyset Indian man with an apron on smoking a cigarette by a dumpster. The man barely seemed to have noticed them, taking one last puff of his cigarette and flicking it into the garbage before going back inside.

Median's phone rang. He didn't recognize the number and realized that didn't matter.

"Six-six-six, six-six-six, six-six, six-six," he said aloud.

"Don't answer that call," Joe said. Median was about to poke the red, 'Ignore Call' button when the green, 'Answer Call' button slid over beneath his thumb just as he pressed down.

"You're about three seconds from me fucking you up the ass!" Rick said.

The chunky Indian guy exploded.

## Chapter 14. – The HOA of the Damned

"What the fuck?" all three of them shouted in unison. Joe hit the windshield wipers, smearing the red and black goo rather than cleaning it off.

"What smells like pop tarts?" Median asked.

"No-no. Not pop tarts," Joe said, wafting the smell toward his face with a wave. "It's more of a strawberry Pillsbury Toaster Strudel."

"It's more of a cherry and we have to get out of here now," Mary said. "Your truck is melting."

She was right. The windshield had completely fogged over, steaming and whatever fruit it was was starting to burn in their noses.

"My truck!" Joe said. He tried to open his door but gooey acid dripped from the door frame. He slammed it back. "Okay."

He put the truck in reverse, the rear view camera coming on. Joe gunned it, peeling out of the alleyway and back onto the street. He continued driving backward, relying on the monitor in the dash to guide him.

Rick continued berating them all on Median's phone. "I so tried to be cool but I'm gonna go full beelzebub on you. The worst thing you could imagine isn't close to what I'm going to do to you. Especially the one who broke my shoulder. Just imagine being one of three hundred people dissecting bodies into four hundred individual pieces. The time it takes to cut up a whole body into one-inch cubic chunks and just when you finish you see you have another body to go and another. A dozen and more."

Mary took the phone from him and powered it off.

"I'd toss it out the window except it won't roll down." She cocked an eyebrow at him and smiled. Median must have had a look on his face because she put her hand over his. "It's going to be okay." She smiled at him. "I know it will."

"Sure," he said.

"He can't kill us. He still needs his baby."

"You mean he can't kill *you*."

That wiped the smile off her face. Median regretted saying it but that was what worried him most. Rick had seemed like such a cool guy but he hadn't been able to beat around the bush enough to assuage his dread regarding how much taking the wrong fetus out of him was going to hurt. How much worse would it be now?

"Median, you have to remember rule number one about the devil," Joe said, whipping the steering wheel around, making Median and Mary lean to one side. "The devil is a liar. No matter how good a thing he promised you it was going to be fucked up somehow. No matter how much worse it seems right now just know it would have been worse had you given him what he wanted."

"You'll have to forgive me if I'm not exactly comforted by that right now," Median said.

They bumped over a curb and a strip of grass and he looked around to see they were in the parking lot of a high school.

"Why are we here?"

"Because we're going to have to get out and run," Joe said. "The front tires blew."

Dusk was coming. Median couldn't tell if they were being followed but the modicum of security he felt inside the truck evaporated.

"I don't want to go out there."

"None of us do," Mary said. "What's the plan, Joe? Break inside the school and try to hold up in one of the classrooms?"

"Uh, yeah. That's exactly what I was thinking."

The truck crawled to a stop in front of the building's front stairs. Joe looked around before sliding his back window open.

"Everybody out!" Joe was long and skinny and he wormed his way through in a second, falling in the flatbed. He turned and held a hand out. Median was broader through the shoulders but he managed his upper body through fine.

His belly was another story.

Somehow it had gotten even bigger.

"I don't think I can make it through!" Median grunted, pushing off the dashboard with his feet. Then he was sliding through and falling into Joe's arms.

"What the hell?" Joe said. Median rolled over as Mary came through a wide opening. "How did you do that?"

"Do what?"

"We don't have time," Mary said, leaping over the side. Joe followed and they held their hands out for Median. He was barely able to lift a leg and almost fell out of the truck. They had to haul him up the stairs.

"Leave me!" Median said. "He doesn't want you. He might leave you alone if he catches me."

"Or he might tear us apart before he does whatever he wants to you." Joe tried scooping him up in his arms. "What have you been eating? You must weigh three hundred pounds!" He quickly put him back down and put one of Median's arms over his shoulders.

They made it all the way up the stairs and to the door. Mary pulled on all the handles and they didn't budge. She peered inside and began waving to someone inside.

Median turned toward the parking lot. It was a lot darker than it should have been at six o'clock. And the street lights weren't on, either. He could spot the truck in the near distance but it looked like it was wading in a puddle of ink. He squinted and thought he could see *things* crawling out of that ink, pulling themselves up the sides of Joe's truck.

"Probably not a good idea to look that way," Joe said.

Several things moaned behind them and Median almost turned to look. Mary and Joe began banging on the doors and Median waddled closer to join them. He couldn't get as close to the doors as he wanted because his stomach was *huge*.

*Did it get bigger since the truck?*

He spied a man inside running a floor buffer. He had on earbuds and was singing along to whatever he was listening to. The moaning grew louder and Median had to resist turning around. There was nothing he could do about whatever was going on behind him. He imagined long, impossibly thin shadows like he'd seen on the truck stretching their way up the stairs, reaching for them.

The security he felt beneath the flood lights was false, if anything, they were a literal spotlight showing exactly where they were, a sort of dinner bell calling the dogs to sup.

Median had to force the thoughts out of his head as the moaning drew closer, an off-key chorus of hungry things poised to devour them.

The floor buffer finally looked up. He took one earbud out and mouthed something at them. They banged on the door even more furiously and he shook his head. He shut his machine off and took his time, shaking out his cord so he didn't trip over it as he meandered toward them.

He pushed into the vestibule and they could hear him speaking but they were banging too intensely on the doors to understand. He stopped in front of one door.

"School's closed!" he shouted.

"Please, let us in!" Mary shouted. "Somebody out here has a gun!"

He looked over their heads toward the parking lot. His mouth dropped open but he didn't speak.

"Please!" she said.

He cracked the door open.

"Anybody call the police?" Joe hooked his fingers on the door and yanked it open. They pushed their way past him and out of the vestibule. Median almost lost his footing on the slick floor but Mary caught his hand.

"Hey, I don't see anybody out there," the floor buffer said. They turned to look at him.

"Shut the door!" Joe said but it was too late. Shadows poured over him and the man's eyes went wide as he was pulled to the floor. His chin cracked against the linoleum.

"Uh—" the man said, as if the precursor to a scream, but a moment later there wasn't enough of him left to make any sound. Shadows swirled around him like attacking bees, disassembling him molecule by molecule.

Joe pushed Median back. "Run. Run!"

Mary got in front, wrenching Median by the arm.

"Ow!" he said but not because of his arm. He had a stitch in his side.

He was able to keep one foot in front of another, staying upright as Joe pushed him from behind and Mary pulled him.

"Ma'am, y'all can't be in here after hours," a tall, lean woman in a blue janitorial uniform said.

"Run," Mary said, grabbing the woman by the sleeve. Rather than running the woman looked in the direction they'd come from.

"Charlie!" she said. "You let this white lady in here?" They kept moving, Mary trying doors at random. The moaning had ceased but they'd been replaced by a sound even more unsettling. The shadows behind them were buzzing, a monotonous tone that was steadily growing louder.

"Is that the alar—" the woman said.

Median looked over his shoulder and was able to catch sight of the woman just before she was pulled apart in thousands of little pieces.

Mary pushed open a door and they followed her into the gymnasium. The basketball rims were all up and to the right of the huge room was a group of people seated in folding chairs in front of a man in a tweed jacket and glasses.

Most of the people looked their way, so many that the man in the tweed jacket stopped talking and turned around to see what they were seeing.

"Excuse me but this is a homeowner's association meeting," he said as they approached. "Is there something I can help you find?"

"No. No," Mary said out of breath. She took a deep gulp of air. The stitch in Median's stomach arched from one side to the other and he fell, the strength sapped from his legs.

"Whoa-whoa-whoa, is he okay?" the tweed jacket man said.

"He's fine," Joe said, panting. "He's just pregnant."

"What?"

Rather than answering, Joe kept walking toward the people seated. Some had gotten up, confused, others were beginning to approach.

"You'd all be better off if you ran," Joe said. "Get as far away from us as you can. Maybe they won't bother with you."

"Who?" an older woman said. But the moaning answered her question as the shadows slid beneath the gymnasium doors.

"Come on, Median," Joe said. "Get up."

"I can't," Median said. "I think I'm gonna shit myself."

"Then shit yourself already and get up."

Median managed to get to his feet as the people looked unsure of what was happening. The tweed jacket man stayed rooted to where he stood, looking toward the doors and not seeing whatever it was moaning.

"I—" he said just before the shadows reached him.

People began screaming once he disintegrated before their eyes. Median managed a few more steps before he tripped. He managed to push Mary and Joe away from him as he went down.

"Median!" Joe said. It was too late. The shadows were on him.

Median felt them swirling over him, cinching around his body. It felt like he was being run through with a pitchfork. He managed to turn around and came face to face with one of the shadows.

With no intention in mind he opened his mouth and bright light shot out. The shadow shook as it was bathed in blinding brightness. Then light heaved out of Median. He vomited it, light brighter than what lit the room pouring out of him, splashing on the floor, burning wherever it touched a shadow.

They retreated from him and Median's whole body convulsed, light shooting out of his pores, shooting to all corners of the room. Moans turned to high-pitched screeches as the remaining shadows sizzled and withered away.

Median was still seizuring on the floor when he heard him, Huey Lewis and the News' 'I Wanna New Drug' playing from somewhere in the gym.

"I always love coming Above. There's such interesting shit up here."

## Chapter 15. Chinchorro

Median was outright exhausted when the seizures stopped. He'd bitten his tongue too.

Rick sauntered over to him and looked down. His arm was in a sling.

"Hey Mary." He waved. "How we doin'?" he asked Median.

"I think…I'm having a baby."

"Yeah. You look like you're about to pop." He clapped his hands and winced in pain. Two lumbering figures joined him, one of them wheeling that same cart from the clinic.

"Don't mind these guys," Rick said. "This is Sujer and Bol. One's a rapist, the other's obsessive compulsive. I make them fuck each other an uneven amount of times." He shrugged. "It works out." He slapped one of the enormous figures on the chest. "I'm doing a kind of Chinchorro thing. Still getting it right." He squeezed the figure's shoulders, molding them and pushing them back. "I don't want to be interrupted this time."

They looked like they'd been assembled out of cardboard boxes. Rudimentary eyes and mouths, no noses, bulky middles, and genitalia that looked like they belonged on some long extinct creature.

"I think you're too late," Median said. "I think the baby's coming now."

"You leave the time up to me."

Median wondered why Mary and Joe weren't doing anything. He looked over and saw they were staring at him. No, not staring. They were frozen in place. Everybody was.

"Look, I tried being reasonable. I'd still be willing to give you what we discussed. But that motherfucker hurt me." He pointed to Joe. "Who is that asshole anyway?"

"That's my roommate." Median was surprised. "Shouldn't you know that?"

"No, I *shouldn't* know that," the devil said. "I told you I'm *hemi*-omnipotent."

He took his time looking over the tools on his tray, tapping an index on his chin.

"Look, wouldn't it be easier to just let the baby come and then start over?" For whatever reason Median felt protective of the life inside him.

"Yeah, it would be. But I can't have two avatars hanging around, can I?"

"Avatars?"

Rick looked away from the tray and at Median on the floor. "You don't know about avatars?"

Median shook his head.

Rick turned and grabbed the heavyset woman who'd come Median's way. He bent her until she was in a seated position and sat in her lap. "Well let me tell you.

"Every devil has an avatar on Earth. A...*representative* of him or herself while toiling in the underworld. It's another way to put the screws to us, y'know, show us what we're missing. People never remember we're also in hell. We're not enjoying ourselves down there. Some of us want to see our avatars lead better lives and maybe get into heaven, some of us root for when our avatars fall on their faces.

"I was looking for something different. Avatars don't have souls so they don't go either way. Once an avatar dies we just get a whole new one. That's supposed to be something good for me." The devil pointed at Median's stomach. "An avatar with an actual soul. An actual person who can make his own life choices and receive his own reward."

"But he could mess up and wind up going to hell," Median said.

"It would be worth it. Got a nice Catholic school picked out, religious parents who would adopt him and take him to church three times a week. I have a whole life mapped out for him. I even have his wife picked out, though. She's three right now."

Median groaned in agony. This baby was kicking the shit out of his kidneys.

"Oo, we better hurry." Rick leaned in close. "How we doin'?"

Median thought he had enough of that light vomit swirling around in his mouth for a loogie. He spat in the devil's face.

"Ugh," he said, taking a big step back. He swiped his eye and wretched several times. "It got in my mouth. Oh my gah—" He wretched again, putting his hands on his knees. He spat. "Sorry, that only works on the lessers." One of his henchmen handed him a handkerchief and he wiped his hand and face. "Oh, I'd better fix what they did while I'm still here." He did a fancy wave with his hand and the man in the tweed jacket reassembled out of thin air.

"The others are restored as well. They technically hadn't done anything for me to claim them prematurely, although if I searched hard enough I'm sure I could probably find something. Lucky for them I don't have the time or the inclination and the last thing I want on my hands is three more souls. Lord knows I certainly don't *need* them."

"*Billy Zane*," Median said. "I just realized you look like Billy Zane."

Rick smiled broadly at him. "Finally, somebody noticed! That's what I was going for when I put this suit together." Rick paused a moment. "Okay, we really need to get started. He grabbed the scalpel thing with the hook at the bottom. "Feel free to scream. I'll be honest, I could have done this painlessly but I don't often get to do something like this to somebody while they're still alive. After I'm done dissecting you I'm going to eat the seed inside and replace it with the one you're supposed to have. Oh, and you'll have a *horrific* scar. You'll look like you survived your own autopsy, only worse."

Then he looked back at the other people in the room as if noticing them for the first time.

"Oh shit. You're all witnesses. Boys, kill them."

The two bulky figures advanced on the members of the homeowner's association, Mary and Joe joined with them.

"You ready?" Rick said, gripping the scalpel in his left hand. "This is probably gonna get really sloppy. I'm a righty."

Median couldn't answer. He was in so much agony all he could do was squirm on the floor. He put his hands to either side of his still expanding belly, wanting to squeeze it like a gigantic zit.

Rick got down on one knee and practiced his swing before he actually plunged the blade into Median. Sujer and Bol kept slowly advancing on the homeowner's association. One man broke away from the group and ran for a set of double doors.

"Dwight!" a woman said. Rick sighed in annoyance and twirled his hand in the air. When the man pushed on one door the push bar flung him backward several feet.

Dwight was grabbed by one of the figures and lifted to his feet. He screamed as it touched one side of his body then the other, going from shoulder to hip to knee.

Then the other one got to him. It punched him, its blocky fist making a hole in the man's torso. His head fell back and the creature began trying to shake his body off it. The first one tried to help, ripping his left arm off, then his right, then his left leg, then his right.

The woman who had screamed for Dwight slumped to the floor but several people pulled her up again.

"We can just keep away from them," Mary said. "They're slow." She tapped Joe on the shoulder. "Lead the way. I'll take the back."

"What about Median?"

"Dammit." Everyone crowded around the two of them. "You just keep herding them around."

She advanced on Rick and Median, clearly seeing the devil raise his arm. Then everything slowed way down.

"She got too close," Rick said. "We're in our own separate bubble of time. A second takes about three hours to pass in here." He smiled. "Oh, I love this solo!" The devil began playing air-sax with the song, his fingers racing up and down the imaginary keys.

Then he stabbed Median in the stomach.

## Interlude 2. Detroit, Michigan October 29th, 1929

A man in a suit ran across the street like he was on fire, one hand full of balled up newspapers, his other firmly on the hat on his head. He ran at me like I wasn't there and I had to step aside to let him pass. He wasn't the only one. White folk all over were running back and forth like they didn't know where they was going. In a few minutes the streets was crowded with 'em like ants or something.

I was wearing one of my nice suits so a nigga on Woodward didn't look too out of place. But it was probly safer to get inside somewhere.

I had to find him first. Alfred.

That...mother*fucker*.

I shouldda choked his ass to death in his crib, consequences be damned.

That looked like his hat about ten yards ahead of me but he might as well have been a mile away. With the sea of people pushing back and forth I was lucky I was still on my feet.

Just then I felt something crunch under my shoe. I looked down just as somebody slapped the hat off my head and saw a man, broken and bloodied, begging me with his eyes.

"Please, sir," the white man said, reaching up with the hand I'd just broken. I saw two of his fingers twisted up, one of them so bad it was like he was pointing at himself.

My mouth fell open. I wanted to reach out to him but just like that he was gone, the heaving crowd almost carrying me off my feet.

I kept my eye open for Alfred's hat and it wasn't hard to spot. A John Bull top hat canted to the side on his big ass head and he was head and shoulders above almost everyone else. I managed to get almost in arm's distance of him but when I tried to reach out to grab him he was gone again. What I managed to do was to sink my hand into the bodice of a lady's dress. I pulled my hand back and was about to apologize when I realized she hadn't noticed.

She'd almost been scalped, the skin that should have been covering the top of her skull flapped over like she was tipping a hat.

I didn't know what was going on but this was a mob turned against itself. These people weren't mad, they were scared and were hurting each other, killing each other.

A fist arced over the head of the man in front of me and hit me square in the mouth. The only reason I didn't go down was the wall of people behind me. I didn't know who'd socked me and right then the only thing I wanted was to get away. I looked around me and saw the crowd had pushed onto the Boulevard. We were near enough to the Henry Ford Hospital campus that I could see the building. It was just my luck to spot Alfred headed that way and I got my feet under me again.

Cars were stopped as the streets were choked with people. One man and his boy stood on the roof of their car, looking down at the crowd, the boy just hung onto his daddy but the look on the man's face said he had no answers for what was happening.

The hospital campus was enclosed by a wrought iron fence. Nobody seemed to be trying to get on the other side of it and I stuck a hand out. I was bigger than most and I'm unashamed to say I knocked over a few people to get against it. The fence was a good eight feet tall and I had just enough strength to climb over top it and fall to the other side. A few people saw and tried to do the same but most of them got knocked back into the crowd and disappeared. One skinny lady got up to the top of the fence but looked too scared to drop over.

"C'mon," I said, waving to her. Something in her eyes said she recognized the color of my skin was a lot darker than hers and she shook her head. "Look, lady, I'll catch you." She shook her head again and made like she would climb back down if I came any closer.

I shook my own head and began looking for Alfred. He was easy enough to spot, tall as me but probly a good thirty pounds lighter. The crowd was just as wild around him but he almost seemed like he didn't notice, taking his time with one hand behind his back and using that cane, strolling more upright than any man should as absolutely none of them touched him.

"You did it, didn't you?" I shouted at him. "You did this."

For a moment I thought he was going to ignore me but he stopped and slowly looked at me. Alfred had skin black as night with green eyes as bright as emeralds. He had a meticulously trimmed beard, his full lips pursed as he decided whether or not to speak to me.

I had to admit he was handsome. Damn, beautiful even. Alfred was sixty-eight years old and didn't look a day over thirty. I was eighty-two but I'd guess I could have passed for twenty-five. I didn't know how or by what process but I knew it was because of him.

"You told me no," he said. His voice was a rich baritone but soft. I'd learned a long time ago to not fall for it. He could control folk he talked to if he wanted. Maybe I'd grown immune to it after being around him so long.

"The white man told me to take care of you. He said you was special, not god," I said. "You gotta turn this off."

Alfred spread his arms.

"If I am not He then I certainly cannot be held responsible."

I rushed at him and grabbed the bars.

"You can't be this petty! These people scared. People gettin' hurt!"

"I am not to be denied. I warned you something like this could happen."

"Dammit! No!"

The thing he'd asked me to do…it was terrible but not like this.

"I'll do it," I said.

He nodded. "Now you do it. *Now* you obey." The smile fell from his face. "Nigga, you too late."

He turned and began his stroll again. I shook the fence, wishing I was strong enough to rip off the bars so I could grab him and tear him limb from limb.

I was strong as about four or five men by my estimate and free from the crowd I could clear this fence. I backed up and looked around. I jumped the fence and came down on top of Alfred. I'd caught him by surprise but that wasn't going to be enough.

"Are you out yo damn mind?" he screamed as we fell to the sidewalk. As strong as I was Alfred was probably stronger. White folk tended to leave him alone but I'd been the punching bag often enough. On the one occasion when four drunk good ole boys decided they wanted to have a go at him Alfred had allowed them the first few punches. He'd even gone down to one knee. They'd thought they had the upper hand but they hadn't seen what I'd seen.

They hadn't seen Alfred smiling the whole time.

He'd let one of them live but without a tongue to tell his story or eyes.

I squeezed his throat, leaning in with my weight hoping to end this as fast as possible. Like him I had killed before but I'd always been sick to death after.

As much as I cursed him, I loved Alfred. I'd raised him since he was a toddler. Cannonade had burnt to the ground and every slave on the plantation knew what that meant. Our days were numbered even though there were just as many colored folk in that house as white folk.

Isis had made it out and she ran with me. The fields were burning, the trees were burning. I saw a horse on fire running down the road. Somehow we survived that night and made our way north, running into Union soldiers by morning.

I'd been too scrawny to fight and wasn't no white soldier gon' take care of no black baby so they gave me directions and some rations. By then I knew I had to keep Alfred safe, no matter what but I'd seen how the northerners were looking at her. She saw how they were looking at her and she knew how important Alfred was. After all, he'd just burnt up her whole family and their livelihood.

"You go on, Milo," she said. "These soldiers'll make sure I get someplace safe."

My tears rained on Alfred's face as I saw Isis one last time in my mind's eye. I'd fooled around and fell in love with a woman I had no right to and hadn't stood for her honor because I'd needed to protect *him*.

107

Those green eyes went wide as his
arrogance gave way, realizing that he *could* die and
that I meant to show him exactly how. He slapped
at me, his hands as big as frying pans as I tucked
my chin to my chest, the blows hitting the top of my
head. I felt the crowd around me change and people
began hitting me. But I'd been in more than my
share of scraps over the last seventy years. I'd been
lynched twice and played dead, hoping they
wouldn't castrate me or set me on fire. I'd been run
through with a pitchfork, shot, bashed on the head
with a shovel, and buried alive in a shallow grave.

I'd endured through all that because of *him*.
I could endure a few dozen limp-wristed white-
collar workers for the next thirty seconds.

He bucked beneath me, the whites of his
eyes going red. He grabbed my wrists but by then
he didn't have the strength to pull me away.
Somebody was hitting me over the head and at
some point I couldn't see from all the tears.
Someone else kicked me in the ribs and I felt the
crunch of Alfred's trachea as it gave way.

I thought protecting him was a mistake
when he was thirteen and he made me sacrifice a
rabbit to him. I skinned it and cooked it up after—
that had made it okay. But he kept wanting more
sacrifices. I never told him about the white man and
the promise I'd made to him. But somehow he knew
he was special. That he was different than other
folk. I tried to teach him to be humble, little as I
knew about humility, but he mistook 'different' for
'superior'.

I knew protecting him all those years was a mistake when he asked me to sacrifice a young girl to him. I'd been on such a track with him for so long that I thought I had to. I took the girl he'd wanted, brought her to the altar I'd built him, and was on the verge of doing it when I saw the look in her eyes.

I…couldn't. I *wouldn't* take her life.

Then he'd done this.

I found out about the stock market crash after and I don't think he caused it. I don't know that his power was that far-reaching. But he took advantage of the panic, spreading it around until he'd created a human stampede. The newspaper later said thirteen people had died and almost a hundred had been injured.

I made sure he was one of the thirteen.

When the life had left his eyes the people stopped attacking me. I slowly looked up and saw they'd stopped doing everything. Everybody was just…frozen. I'd just taken a man's life and knew they wouldn't waste time pointing fingers. Alfred was—had been—mine and I'd done the best I could with him. I'd had to take him out the world even though I hadn't brought him in it.

I kissed his forehead, tears staining his face. I closed his eyes and stood, feeling every minute of my eighty-two years.

It was three months before the white man came. I hadn't run, I knew he'd come no matter where I went. I'd made my home here and intended to die on my terms and not like some animal.

"Milo," he said on the other side of the door to my apartment. All these years later and the voice was exactly how I remembered. I shouldn't have been surprised considering how old I was but he'd looked forty-something way back then. He could have been younger, I suppose—white folk always look older'n they are to me.

I opened the door and there he was, tall and gaunt, only this time I was taller than him. But I felt like I was that little boy all over again, Man-man wondering who that was coming to Cannonade.

"May I come in?" The way he was swathed up in bandages was different. He was more covered than the before. I wanted to ask if he was all right but something told me not to acknowledge how he looked. A few years later I'd gone to see *The Mummy* with a girlfriend and Imhotep had reminded me of the white man. It was the scariest thing I'd ever seen.

I stood back for him to come in. He…glided. When I looked down to see if he had feet all I could see was swirling robes.

"So…you've killed him." He had his back to me, looking around my little apartment.

"Yes sir, I did."

"Did you see to it that he was buried properly?"

"I did."

The white man began pulling at one of his gloves as he nodded. "Good. Good."

He didn't seem angry. I recalled the night Benton had died and the hodgepodge story I'd gotten about Adolph and figured I was about to be as dead as Reggie.

The white man turned around and looked at me. Well, I assume as much but he had on dark glasses so I couldn't see his eyes. He held his hand up for me to see—if that's the word that applies, that is. His hand had no color to it. Not white—absolutely no color at all. I could see his hand and I could also see through it clearly.

So this was how it was to be. Without another word he glid over to me and touched my cheek with that hand. I won't lie and say I didn't jump back but when he touched me I felt a tremendous sense of...comfort.

"You...have done well, Milo. I love you."

"What, sir?"

He shook his head, his whole body quaking with silent laughter. "All this time and you never figured it out. You never *knew*."

"Knew what, sir?"

"It was always you. Alfred wasn't the one I chose. It was you. Alfred was simply the test. I had to know how far you could be pushed. When you would make your own decision."

"Excuse me, sir?"

"Oh, don't get me wrong. He had power. But his power he drew from you. If you ever felt weaker than him it was because you allowed it."

I didn't understand then. It took several days for me to take what he'd said in. "But why?" I asked.

"Because," he said.

"What do you mean 'because'?" Anger had finally crept into my words. That was the reasoning of a child. 'Because' wasn't a reason.

The white man laughed out loud. He laughed so hard he bent over and clutched his middle. He laughed so long I was on the verge of laughing myself.

"There are a great many pieces to this grand puzzle, my boy." He put his hands on my shoulders. "If I gave you an actual reason you would be just as flummoxed as you are now." He put his hat back on his head and headed for the door. "The time will come when you believe you have a greater understanding. Maybe you will be right, maybe you won't. Act."

He opened the door and stepped into the hallway.

"I suspect you will never see me again. My time here has been so…brief. I love you so *much*, Milo."

I watched him glide down the hallway and disappear around the corner.

He didn't have feet.

## **Chapter 16. And Baby Makes Three**

"Aw, what the fuck?" Rick said and tossed another broken blade to the floor. "That's what I get for buying this shit in China." He stood and put his hand on his hip as he thought. The people kept running around, Sujer and Bol mindlessly—and slowly—pursuing them.

*Such dumbasses*, he thought. *If they split up they could catch them.*

"Would you like some help?"

Rick looked around and saw an old black dude just standing there. The guy looked like he was ninety years old, the boys could have gotten him easy.

"What are you gonna do, old timer?"

"Seems to me that young man is about to have a baby. Yours?"

"No. And he wants to have an abortion. I'm just trying to help him out."

The old dude shrugged and started walking toward them. "I think I understand what's going on," he said. "You're a devil. And not one of those freaky little robot ones, right?"

That got Rick's attention. He could *see*. What's more he'd seen those other devils. Those things gave even him the creeps. They'd been made back in the 1950s and after malfunctioning spectacularly had mostly been rounded up and destroyed.

"Stay back, old fella. I, uh…I got this."

"Nah, you don't. You probly got this whole thing upside down."

"What?"

The old man nodded. "If anybody could get a man pregnant he'd have to be god or devil. Right?"

"Uh, yeah."

"I doubt a god would even be interested. I mean, they haven't impregnated a human being in about two thousand years."

This guy was making a lot of sense. Rick probably could have figured out this stuff on his own had he just sat down and thought about it, though. One of the other devils probably did this. Maybe Greg, Jeff—ooo, maybe that asshole Jose.

The old man held up a finger. "It wasn't anybody else. It was you."

"What? No. The guy I sent screwed up. He didn't make it in time and somebody else was there."

"There…is nobody else. Do you understand?"

Rick made a face. What the hell was this guy talking about?

"You *are* the devil. *The* devil. The boys upstairs played a nasty trick on you." He crossed into the time bubble and didn't freeze like the girl had. "People don't think about the fact the devil is also in hell. It's just as much a torment for you as anyone else. And making you believe you are being pursued by other devils—by *you*—is just another way of putting the screws to you."

"Hey. Back off." This old guy was freaking Rick out.

"That's your baby. You just don't remember."

"Mine?" Rick guffawed. "No-no-no."

"That's why you can't destroy him. The part of you that knows won't allow it."

Rick gave him the finger and tapped his chest. "I don't get mindfucked. I *do* the mindfucking."

"Look at the knife you just tossed on the floor. Really look at it."

Rick glanced down at the knife at his feet. He'd broken it trying to cut Median open but there it was, *not* broken. He knelt and picked it up. Rick held it in his hand then looked up at the old man.

"Anybody ever tell you you look like Louis Gossett, Jr.?"

"Get up." The old man helped him to his feet. He might have looked frail but he was really strong. They both looked down at Median. He was squirming around and moaning on the floor. Like a little bitch.

"What do we do now?" Rick asked.

"We get ready to welcome your baby into the world.

## **Chapter 17. My Two Da-das**

"Being Above requires that I accurately represent myself when on official business."

"And on unofficial business?"

Rick shrugged. "There is no such thing as unofficial business. Unofficial means I have no business being here. I conduct my business then I go back Below. Think of this as going to a work conference and stopping to pick up dry cleaning on the way home."

"I'm your starched shirts?"

"Exactly." Rick clapped his hands together. The three men stood together in a pool of light. It looked a lot like a gymnasium swimming pool but instead of water it was filled with milky, liquid fluorescence. Median's feet were swept from beneath him and he was floating on his back.

"How bad is this going to hurt?" Median asked.

"Not sure, really, probably a little at least. Sorry about before. I mean, I could have done this from the start. Old habits, y'know."

"No, it's cool. So how does this start?"

"You just relax and…let it go," the old man said.

"Hm." Median nodded. "Who are you?"

"My name's Milo. I'm one of the people your friend here was about to tear apart. Oh and can you—"

"Oh, yeah-yeah-yeah-yeah." Rick snapped his fingers. "Done. Everything back to normal."

Median couldn't see the devil side of Rick and something told him that wherever they were wasn't exactly real. He looked at his swollen belly and rubbed it one last time.

"Okay. So I just let go. Do I need to—I dunno—push or something?"

"Just let go," Milo said.

Median didn't know what that meant but he concentrated. His stomach lit up, the skin translucent. He could see *something* stirring around in there and it began moving down…down. . .

"And there we go," Milo said.

"Was that it?" Median said. "It was just a pinch. I don't get what all the fuss is about."

"Where is he? Where is he?" Rick could barely contain his excitement. He splashed about in the light, looking for his baby.

116

"He's all around us," Milo said. "We've been inside him all this time. Well, 'him' would be inaccurate. Calling a baby an 'it' just seems wrong."

"I wanna see my baby. I wanna hold him— it. I don't care what."

"Hey, it's my baby too," Median said, looking around.

"Well, if he wants he can take a physical form."

Rick turned to him. "Why do you know so much, old timer?"

Milo shrugged. "Because."

Light rose from the pool and began taking shape. Rick clapped his hands excitedly.

It took the general form of a child about four years old. A pair of eyes opened and it looked down on the three of them. Rick waded over to it and grabbed its foot.

"Hey, buddy," he said. "I'm your da-da! Can you say da-da?"

"Me too!" Median waded over and touched the other foot. "I'm your da-da too! Say da-da to me!" It looked at the both of them then at Milo.

"Hey, why's he looking at you?"

"I think you know, Rick."

"No. No, man. I just got here. I haven't gotten to spend any time with him!"

"You wanted some aspect of you that was untainted, right? What happens the longer you stay with him?"

"I know." Rick splashed the light in the pool.

"So he's coming with me then?" Median said.

"No. You're barely any better than him." Milo nodded at Rick.

"Then who? You?"

Milo nodded.

"Wait. Why you?"

"Because...because I'll kill him if that's what's needed."

Median and Rick stared at him.

"I'd like to think that I've gained a lot of wisdom in my hundred and fifty or so years on this Earth. I can avoid the mistakes I made before."

"Why would he choose you?" Rick asked.

"Because we met before." Milo smiled. He rose out of the light and floated over to the white baby. They joined hands and slowly rose toward the ceiling.

"This is bullshit," Rick said.

## Chapter 18. Bye-bye Beelzebub

Median jolted awake on the gymnasium floor with Rick standing over him. Mary took two steps and connected with a right cross that sent the devil to the floor. She wasted no time mud-stomping him, his head bouncing off the wooden floor as she attacked.

"Mary!" Median said, standing. "Mary!" She finally relented and looked at her husband as he patted down his flat stomach.

"What? What happened?" she said.

"I think it already happened," he said. "I think it came out." The memory was already fading like it had been a dream.

"Well that's just one less step for me!" Rick stood and staggered over. He wiped blood on his white jacket. "Make room for Daddy!"

Median hoped the devil wasn't about to try to rape him.

"Whoa-whoa-whoa," Median said. "We're talking artificial insemination, right?"

"Yeah," Rick said. "I'm not gay or nothin'. Unless you're into that sort of thing."

"Okay, so where's the stuff?"

Rick made a face like he didn't understand.

"Where's the stuff? Y'know…the stuff?"

Rick realized what he was talking about and began patting down his pockets. "Aw, dammit, did either of you guys bring the stuff?" He kicked a chair in frustration and it got hung up on his foot. "Shit!" he said. "Shit! Shit! *Shit!* I came all this way and you idiots forgot the stuff! Now we gotta go all the way back home and—ugh! I'm just gonna call the whole thing off. It is a pain in the ass to get up here once, I'm not making two trips."

Sujer and Bol lumbered over and stood behind Rick.

"We out. Losers." He flashed the peace sign and snapped his fingers. They were gone in a plume of black smoke. Just before Median had made eye contact with him. He couldn't be sure but wherever he'd been he thought Rick had been there too and something in the devil's eyes had seemed…aware.

119

Joe came over, coated in sweat and breathing heavily.

"Hey, what happened to that old guy?"

## Chapter 19. Let's Get Pancakes

They'd dropped Mary off at home despite her protests. Median felt guilty enough with her risking her life for him (despite her being part of the reason his life was at risk anyway). He'd promised to call when they were done.

There were several points along the way where Joe could have left him behind and nobody could have blamed him. In fact, helping Median had even cost Joe his truck. He owed Joe for sticking his neck out the way he had. Or at least that was what he figured after Joe told him he did.

The three of them had taken an Uber back to Mary's place and then Joe and Median had borrowed Mary's car. He'd taken the time to reassure Mary that everything was going to be fine.

"Why do you even need to go see this guy?" she'd asked.

"He stole something of Joe's from my car. He left a note for us to meet so he can get it back."

She'd made a face at him and he knew what that had meant. It didn't make sense. If the guy was telling them where he was going to be, they should have called the police to arrest him. Median hadn't said—and Mary hadn't asked—why exactly it was that they couldn't call the police. He could see the exhaustion in her eyes and Median wanted to just curl up and go to sleep too. In fact, he could have done so right here on her doorstep.

But Joe leaning on the horn had reminded him that wasn't an option.

Median had kissed her on the cheek and jogged to the car.

"Okay, here's the game plan," Joe had begun. "You're gonna drop me off two blocks before you get to Jefferson. You keep on and I'll catch up. I'll creep up on the situation, crack the guy over the head—we go get pancakes."

"You know it's not going to be that easy," Median said.

Joe sighed. "Yeah, I know. A guy can dream."

"I like the idea of the pancakes, though," Median said. He could almost taste them. As a matter of fact he could smell the melting butter and see the honey maple syrup as it poured from a warm bottle.

He'd only taken his eyes off the road for a moment. Honest.

But the truck that smashed into them had Median seeing hotcakes that didn't flip right. You know the kind—you shovel your spatula under them but they're not done enough and they wrinkle and ooze and once that happens they're just no good and you just have to scrape the whole thing into the sink and start again.

## Chapter 20.

"You mooks can wake up now."

I'm not so much concerned by the other one but Walker Harris I pour a nice drink of water over his head. He comes to trying to flap his arms and legs but he's secured to his chair.

I found a remote place for us to have a chat before I do the deed. Harris' gift got me thinking a little bit more about the kind of man he is. Maybe the angel doesn't know. Maybe sending him to the angel might be a mistake.

When he's gathered enough of his marbles he looks at me. I bothered to take his present out the box and put it within eyeshot.

"I've been talking to our mutual friend," I say.

He looks as me, anxious as a monkey with a can of bananas.

"I don't know what you're talking about," he says. I nod, I respect him more for lying to me. It would be too easy for him to just tell me everything I want to know. He's making me work for it.

"I know who you really are. I know why you're here." I'm bluffing but acting like I know more than I do has worked for me more times than it hasn't.

"I don't know what you mean. I came because of the note you left in my car. You broke my window and stole a box. I think it had a birthday cake in it."

He looks at his partner but that one is still out. He's in bad shape. Broken wing.

"We both know that ain't nothing anybody wants at a birthday party." I step aside so he can see the head. "Me and your friend have been talking," I say.

"Talking?" he asks. By the look on his face he knows the jig is up.

## Chapter 21. Where Angels Live

"Don't listen to him," the head said. "He's crazy."

Median didn't know exactly how to take that. A decapitated head telling him that a man was crazy wasn't exactly a rousing endorsement for his own sanity. He *wanted* to ask what this guy was talking about but he couldn't exactly ask aloud.

The man looked familiar, though. Median thought he might have seen him on TV or something.

"He snatched me out the car," the head said. "And ever since he's been talking to himself. Sometimes he talks like I've been talking back to him but I haven't said a word. For real!"

Median nodded to let the head know he'd understood. He needed to figure out how to get out of this situation and the head might have been key to figuring that out. The ropes were really tight and they were chafing his wrists.

"You know the angel wanted me to deliver you to him," he said. Median had no idea what he was talking about. "But I don't know if you're worthy. I mean, you have decapitated heads in your car, for crying out loud. Killing you might be a mistake."

Median wanted to say that killing him would absolutely be a mistake but he didn't want to throw this guy off his track just yet. He didn't even know what he wanted, let alone how to get himself out of this situation.

Mary was going to be so mad if he died tonight. And who was the angel for chrissake?

"Who is the angel?" Median figured that was a safe enough question.

"Only the sweetest, most beautiful creature any of mankind could ever hope to lay their peepers on. He wanted me to bring you to him. To kill you."

"Wait, what? How can you bring me to him if you kill me?"

"Where do angels live?" The crazy asshole pointed skyward.

"Okay, that's a fair point. But how do you know killing me wouldn't have sent me to hell?"

"That's a fair point. Maybe I should kill you." He slid a cannon of a gun out of a shoulder holster. It was a weird moment for déjà vu but Median definitely knew this guy from somewhere.

"Then how would you bring me to this angel?"

The man paused. "Maybe...maybe I shouldn't bring you to him. Maybe there's somebody better."

"Somebody better?" Median asked. "Who?"

"*Me.*"

Median didn't know exactly how to handle this guy but he was certain he was off his rocker.

"I vote for an independent judge," Median said. He wasn't exactly sure where he was going but it got the man to stop coming closer with that gun. "What's your name anyway?"

"Hammercock."

"Hey, I know you. You're the guy from that eighties TV show. I used to watch that every Sunday when I was a kid."

Hammercock's face fell. "That was not an appropriate show for children. There was suggestive language, violence, and some sexual situations."

"I know but it was funny. I watched the first few episodes with my parents before Matlock."

"Hey! Hey!" the head said. "I have an idea. Tell him you want Scooby Doo Court."

Hammercock had said something he'd missed.

"What?" Median said.

"I said your parents were bad. No wonder you wound up here."

"Scooby Doo Court. Trust me."

Median felt like he was diving into an empty pool. "Scooby Doo Court!" he shouted.

"What?" Hammercock asked.

"You heard me."

"Tell him to take out one of those gold coins in his pocket."

"You have some gold coins in your pocket. Take one of them out."

"How do you know—" Hammercock narrowed his eyes, although he did as he was told.

"Tell him to wave it around in the air."

"Hold it up. Wave it around."

"Oh! Whistle! Tell him to whistle too."

"And whistle."

"I don't know how to whistle."

"Tell him to fake it."

"Just fake whistle."

Hammercock lifted an eyebrow but held the coin up in the air. "Phweeeeeeeee!" he said. "Phwee-phweeeeeeee!" He turned back to Median. "What is this supposed to do?"

Before Median could answer a dog began trotting toward them. He didn't know where they were but suspected this was either an abandoned building or one still under construction. Median didn't know dogs. This one was medium-sized and looked like some sort of mutt—its front was grey with black spots, its hindquarters a solid brown. It looked like it had been assembled out of two different dogs.

"Tell him to give the dog the coin."

"Give the coin to the dog."

"No way!" Hammercock held the coin to his chest.

"You can't seriously think you should be going by your own judgment," Median said. "You're insane. Give it to the dog."

Hammercock looked between the Median and the dog, sitting patiently on the floor in front of him, tongue lolling. He gave Median a last suspicious glance before holding the coin out for the dog.

It leaned forward, sniffed at the coin then took it gently between its teeth and began chomping on it. The coin broke into pieces and for a moment Median worried it was one of those chocolate coins covered in gold foil. But then he was relieved to see it was gold throughout.

The dog coughed once and chewed the rest of the coin up and swallowed it. The dog licked its chops then sat, looking up at Hammercock again.

"Now what?" he asked. Median looked at the head.

"Just wait," the head said.

The dog sneezed. It shook its head like it had something in its nose. Then it sneezed again.

"Bless you," Hammercock said.

"Thank you," the dog said. The man jumped back in surprise.

His mouth hung open and he looked at Median. "You did this."

"No, you did. You called the dog and gave it the coin from your pocket." He licked his lips, nervous but having a good idea where he was headed. "That dog is an impartial juror. Let him decide what happens next."

"Her," the dog said. "My name is Mai."

Mai had dragged over another chair while Hammercock and Median were talking. She hopped up in it, her posture honorable if not regal.

"I'm ready to hear your arguments," she said.

## Chapter 22. Scooby Doo Court

They both recounted the story to her, filling in for one another and making corrections until they'd gotten to this point. The dog looked back and forth between them.

"What evidence do you have that this was an angel?" she asked Hammercock.

"I told you. He was beautiful. I'd never seen anything like him."

"Do you frequently obey what beautiful people tell you to do?"

"No. Usually, I tell the dames what's what?"

"Probably thirty years ago," Median said.

"Order!" Judge Mai said.

"Sorry, Your Honor."

"He gave me these." Hammercock took three gold coins out of his pocket and held them up. There's an angel right on them. The judge shook her head.

"That's not evidence of anything. How do you know he wasn't a pretty thief?"

Hammercock looked offended by the question. "Because he was an angel."

"Mr. Hammercock, I have no doubt of the sincerity of your beliefs but you did you verify this angel's identity at all?"

"Angels don't carry ID."

"Then I'm afraid—"

"Wait, you haven't verified this devil character he was talking about!"

"I don't think that's germane to the matters at hand. You have failed to establish that you have been deputized by any Holy authority or otherwise authorized to work on its behalf." She looked at Median. "Sir, you are free to go with the apologies of this court. Release the defendant."

Hammercock turned red in the face. "*No.*"

"Excuse me?" Judge Mai said.

"You have no authority over me. I don't acknowledge this kangaroo-dog court." He reached for his gun again and Mai barked. She was out of the chair before he had his gun out and chomped down on his thigh.

Median yanked furiously at his ties but they were really on there. He looked over at Joe who was only starting to come awake. He wondered briefly if it were better to be awake or asleep before being murdered.

Hammercock screamed as he pointed. The problem with that big ass gun was he couldn't really point it at the dog because the barrel was so long. Mai went on tearing at him, pulling away a long strip of his trousers and diving back in at his pale thigh.

He fired, the gun like booming thunder inside this place. Median looked, worried he would see Mai separated into two half dogs. But she was still there, chomping away at his leg. Hammercock's gun was gone and he was slapping at her snout until she yelped and jumped back.

"You're part of it," Hammercock said, pointing at her. "I should have known."

Mai barked and lunged at him. He grabbed for her and she went under him, snapping at his ankle. He turned but wasn't fast enough to catch her. Mai danced away from him, remaining within a few feet. He pursued her, limping badly, and she backed away.

Hammercock was too old and slow to catch Mai but when he picked up a piece of brick Median's heart sank. She barked at him and danced around but the old man took his time. He waited, walking her down until she'd mistakenly backed into a corner. He threw the brick, bouncing it off her skull. Mai fell over and he scooped her up.

"Don't hurt her!" Median shouted. He looked at the head. "Do something!"

"Like what?"

To his relief, Hammercock put her in another room and shut the door. He staggered back toward Median and Joe who was finally coming aware.

"What the hell is Hammercock doing here?" he asked. "Ow, my arm." Joe had taken the brunt of the vehicle crashing into them. He had to have a concussion and the laceration on his scalp had been oozing steadily.

Hammercock found his gun, picked it up and aimed at Median.

"Whoa, why is Hammercock about to shoot you!"

"Long story," Median said. "But he thinks an angel wants him to kill me."

"Is that true?" Joe asked.

"Don't worry. I've got a ticket to hell for you too."

"Is that a yes?"

Hammercock nodded.

"No, it isn't. He said the angel told him to bring me to him."

"You think the angel wanted the baby too?"

"No idea. I don't even know who the angel supposedly is."

"Shut up!" Hammercock said. "What baby?"

"Until a little bit ago Median here was pregnant."

"Liars. Both of you." Hammercock raised his gun.

"Wait-wait-wait!" Joe said. "If you're supposed to kill him wouldn't the angel have told you that specifically?" Hammercock didn't shoot. "I mean, what if he just wanted to tell him he won a prize or something?"

Median looked at him, confused.

"What I'm saying is if he wanted Median alive for some purpose and you just kill him, won't that piss him off?"

Hammercock's aim wavered.

"At the very least would it hurt anything to just wait until this angel character got here?"

By the confused look on his face Median thought Joe had gotten through to him. He just hoped this angel didn't have something worse in mind.

## Chapter 23. The Gray Man

To summon him Hammercock took something out of his pocket that looked like a rock. He rubbed his thumb over it and put it back.

"It shouldn't be long," he said.

The temperature dropped what felt like twenty degrees. Median wasn't sure how but he felt a presence. Then he heard footsteps.

"He's coming." The older man looked giddy. It was very unsettling.

A tall figure appeared next to Hammercock.

"I am the angel," he said. Everybody looked at him.

He was…gorgeous.

He had to have been about six-foot seven with skin that looked like it had been carved out of onyx, a pronounced jaw, blond goatee, and the biggest, greenest eyes Median had ever seen.

He wore a tailored gray suit and crossed the floor to get a closer look at Median. Median would have given him absolutely anything he asked for.

"I…I found him for you, angel."

"Yes. Yes, you did." His voice was a rich baritone but soft. Not much above a whisper yet powerful enough to cut through a noisy room.

"That's not an angel," the head said. Median barely heard him.

"May I have my reward now?" Hammercock asked. Despite apparently being the oldest person in the room he sounded like a child.

"Your…reward?" He looked at the older man. "Did I not compensate you?"

"Yes, but. . ."

"Say it."

"I was hoping I could come with you, angel."

"Ah." The angel laughed. "I see. Of course. As a matter of fact, you can go ahead of me. Prepare a place for us."

Hammercock looked around, confused. The angel smiled and the tension seemed to drain out of the older man. He smiled too and nodded.

Then he ran straight for the nearest window and jumped out.

"Oh shit!" the head said. "Median, you have to snap out of it. If you can scooch over to Joe maybe the two of you can help each other out."

Something banged in the distance and a car alarm began sounding.

"Now that we're done with that distraction," the angel said. He looked at Joe. "Unless you're going to be a problem?"

"No." Joe shook his head. "Not at all."

"What...do you want?" Median asked.

"Sacrifice."

"I don't have the baby anymore."

"No, you don't. But you still have the womb."

"I...do?"

"Yes. And Joe has all the parts I asked him to collect."

"That was you?" Joe asked.

"*Yes.*"

There were more footsteps approaching, bare feet.

"Oh my god," the head said.

Median saw the figure approaching. Naked and headless.

"And now I have the final two pieces."

"Median! Median, listen to me. Ask him what he's going to do."

"What...are you gonna...do?"

The angel looked intrigued. "I didn't think you'd be interested. Well, let me introduce you." He waved his fingers for the headless figure to approach. It stood next to him and Median saw the body was composed of hodgepodge of several bodies, male, female, many different skin tones.

"Whoa," Median said.

"I have sustained myself over the last ninety years by sacrifice. But I want more. I want something that will sustain me indefinitely. I want my own avatar...in heaven."

"How will you do that?"

"That's right, Median, wake up," the head said.

"By sacrificing my sacrifices all over again. Except I'll add that womb inside you. The life I take then will suffuse me beyond my capacity. The only place for the excess energy to go...is up."

"Wait, how do you know that?"

"That's my boy!" the head said.

"What?" the angel said.

"I mean, how do you know that will work?"

"Because I've learned. . ." the angel sounded insecure. "I've studied the human soul for decades. I taught myself how to absorb the life energies of others."

"But have you ever done *this*?"

"No, not exactly."

"Then you don't know that it will work. For all you know it could give you a really bad case of diarrhea."

"I see you have worked free of my effect." He seized Median by the throat. "No matter. I don't need *you*. Only your womb."

The angel snapped his fingers. The headless body was holding onto a case. It opened the case and sat it on the floor. All manner of blades were inside.

"Oh boy, not this again."

"What?"

"Rick did this earlier. It didn't work. Some old guy helped me give birth."

"Some old guy?" The angel stared into Median's eyes. "What did he look like?"

"I don't know." Median shrugged in his chair. "Old."

"Black or white?"

"Black."

"Big guy? Tall?"

"He looked like he might have played football a long time ago."

"Did he tell you his name?"

"I think so. I can't really remember. I think I was dreaming when I gave birth and he was there too. If that makes sense."

"All this time." The angel looked frightened. "He might have booby-trapped you."

"Oh, cool, so you're gonna let me go then?"

"No. I need that womb. I just won't be killing you to get it." He knelt over the case on the floor and fished around.

"Hey, what's your name, by the way?" Median asked. "Unless it really is 'The Angel'."

The angel stood and turned around with a long, tube-thing in his hand connected to a thing with a trigger. "You may call me…Alfred."

## Chapter 24. A Sort of Handjob

It wasn't exactly a painful process. It was more uncomfortable and very undignified. It involved him taking off his pants and underwear and he would just as much have preferred that nobody knew much more than that.

The womb swirled around in a glass container. Alfred smiled, holding it up in one hand. He and the headless body had untied him and tied him down again on the floor. But they weren't as good as Hammercock and Median thought he could get at least one of his hands out.

"So how is this going to work?" he asked.

"I put the womb into the sacrifice then sacrifice. Well, not me. Joe will do it. Just like he did all the others."

Joe was untied too. And holding a big ass, wicked looking knife. He was still under Alfred's spell.

"Do you want him to slit your throat now or after?"

"Um. After?"

Alfred picked the head up and held it over the body.

"I don't have a good feeling about this," the head said. "If I do anything weird after this I'm sorry."

Black liquid reached up from the open neck and began attaching to the head. Its eyes rolled up as Alfred moved it around until he had it placed to his satisfaction. He picked up the womb, considered it a moment, then pushed the head's chin down, opening the mouth. He put the mouth of the bottle to the lips and poured the womb out.

The body lay on the floor next to Median. Alfred waved Joe over and had him straddle the legs. Median had just managed to get his hand free and no one had noticed. If they were about to do this now then he didn't have much time to make his move. He definitely didn't know what he was supposed to do. If only he could wake the head up to tell him.

Then he knew.

## Chapter 25. Shooting Thick Ropes

Median was going to have to strike quickly. Alfred was a few feet away but he'd be on top of him fast and Joe was next to him with that knife in his hands, seemingly oblivious to the pain of his broken arm.

He balled his fist. He took a big gulp of air and held it. Then he struck.

He twisted as fast as he could and punched the head in the head, hoping to dislodge it from the body. Median figured separating it from the body would bring it back and maybe it would have a last ditch suggestion that would save the day.

But that punch was a helluva punch. It sounded like a shotgun blast. Alfred hit the floor, clutching his shoulder. Median saw the panic in his eyes.

"Do it!" he shouted. "Do it now!"

What was better than one explosion punch? Two explosion punches. Median aimed for Joe's balls and swung. He connected but Joe didn't seem to notice, instead plunging the knife into Median's arm.

Median screamed and yanked away, the knife still in him.

Then Mary was there. Holding a shotgun. She racked it and pointed at Alfred. He was fast, leaping off the floor just as she shot, tearing a hole in the floor where he'd been a millisecond before. She kept racking and firing as he dodged from side to side, getting closer and closer to her.

All Median could do was cradle his arm. It didn't hurt just yet and he was sure it would start bleeding any second. Wait, he was cradling his arm. That meant his other arm was free too. He looked up and saw Joe on his back, unconscious again and the body was gone.

Alfred batted the shotgun aside as Mary fired one last time.

The body was running up behind Alfred.

It plunged two of the blades from the case into Alfred's back. He let Mary go and yelled. He spun around and with one blow knocked the body into several pieces. Most of the upper torso was still together and the arms clapped to either side of the head, the head screaming as they yanked it off and threw it Alfred.

"I have meaning beyond exposition!" it screamed, arcing through the air and landing mouthfirst beneath his chin. Alfred grunted, grabbing the head and wrenching it off. He flung it away like a bowling ball but the damage had been done.

He felt his neck and looked surprised to find his throat was gone. He thrashed around, punching the wall behind him and stalking around aimlessly as he bled profusely. Actually, blood hosed out of him, way more than should have been in one human body. Alfred's green eyes settled on Median and he pointed at him.

Or at the knife.

Median yanked at the ties on his ankles and his hands were too clumsy to untie them. Shit, he was going to have to do it. He slashed at the them with the blade where it came through his arm. The first one snapped fast and he moved to the other.

He saw Alfred's big foot just in time and rolled out the way. But he still wasn't free. Alfred coughed, swayed, then turned on him. Median sawed at the tie, then stood up when Alfred took a step toward him.

He tried to run as the much bigger man reached for him and was pulled off his feet by the last shred of the tie on his ankle. It had snapped, though, and he was able to put space between him and Alfred.

His big green eyes burned with determination as he stomped toward Median. He didn't see Mary as she hooked his leg with her ankle and he went down. He bounced back to his feet and kept coming but a lot of the fight had been taken out of him. Median was easily able to outpace him as Alfred followed him around.

Alfred had been staggering but now he began slipping in his own blood. The entire front of his gray suit was coated in blood and he left big red footprints as he walked.

His throat wound had reduced to steady streaming by the time he fell to one knee. Alfred rose slowly, shuffled forward a few inches, then reached for him. Then he fell on his face.

Blood pooled underneath him as they waited several minutes. Finally, Mary nudged him over with her boot, shotgun reloaded.

"Damn, you're still alive, aren't you?"

Median came close enough to see. His green eyes were still alert but the only thing that could have been keeping him alive now was force of will.

"Killing you would be a mercy."

"No, wait," Median said. "I don't know if he can die. Not like normal people. I think—" he looked at the knife still in his arm. It still didn't hurt but it throbbed in time with his pulse. About six inches of the blade poked out the other side of his arm.

"Then do it."

"Just a minute, Sarah Connor," Median said.

Joe joined them, holding his head and pointed to Median's lower body.

"What the hell is going on?" he asked. "And why are you Porky Pigging it?"

"I don't want to talk about it right now." Median pulled his shirt down as much as he could.

Median braced himself and counted three. He held his arm over Alfred's face. He couldn't do it, though.

"Okay, I'll do it." Mary reached for the knife.

"No!" Median said. "It's keeping me alive right now."

"It wouldn't matter anyway," somebody else in the room said.

All three of them looked around to see who had spoken.

## Chapter 26. Where are My Pants? Part II

The head was still alive.

It took them a good two minutes to find it, but there it was beneath a pile of drywall.

"He sort of can't die anymore," the head said once Median had dusted it off.

"That head is talking?" Joe said, amazed. "I knew there was a reason I took it."

"No, you didn't," the head said. "You were half mesmerized by Alfred. Median, where are your pants?"

"I don't want to talk about it," Median said. "Could you guys help me look for my pants?"

"Median, do you know this head?" Mary asked.

"Um, sort of. It was in the fridge. Joe put it there."

"It wasn't my fault as has been previously established." Joe held up an index to bring his point home.

"So what do we do?" Median asked.

"We feed him through a meat grinder," Mary said.

"Won't work. It would take longer but he would just come back eventually."

"We quarter him, leave one section of him here and the three of us scatter into the wind, never to see one another again as we take our respective pieces to the far corners of the Earth."

Mary and Median looked at Joe.

"Promising but it probably wouldn't work. Eventually, you'll die and the pieces would somehow find their way back to one another."

"Launch him into the sun?" Joe said.

"You have a rocket?" Mary asked.

"Hey, I seem to be the only one coming up with any suggestions here."

"I called for the meat grinder."

"And the head said it wouldn't work. By the way, how are you talking?"

The head almost seemed to shake itself. "I dunno. At first Median was the only one who could hear me. Something about how Alfred set up the sacrifice must have brought me back."

"What did he do?" Mary asked.

"Nothing special, I don't think," Median said.

"He catheterized Median and drew the womb out of him." Median's cheeks flushed. "I don't completely understand it but he believed sacrificing an already sacrificed body would give him an avatar in heaven."

"Would that have actually worked?"

The head seemed to shrug. "Not sure. Don't really think it matters now."

"Wait." Median turned to look at Alfred on the floor and the remains of the body. "You said he's not dead, right?"

"Not all the way."

"Here, hold this." He handed the head to Mary who looked like she would vomit or scream, depending on whichever one came out of her mouth first. He walked over to where the pieces of body were, lying in three separate hunks. It didn't take him long to find it and Median grabbed the bottle Alfred had temporarily stored the womb in. He squeezed a section that either had part of an armpit or a thigh until the glowing womb oozed out, catching it in the bottle again.

"What are you gonna do with that?" Joe asked.

"I'm going to finish what he started." Median walked over to where Alfred's body lay which had started twitching. His eyes rolled around in his head and Median figured the mostly dead man must have guessed what he was up to.

He was able to keep his mouth closed and Median realized that didn't matter. He sat on Alfred's chest and poured the womb into his open throat and then began massaging it down. In seconds it had disappeared all the way inside him.

"Does anybody know if there are supposed to be appropriate words to a sacrifice?"

Mary and Joe both looked at the head.

"Don't look at me, I was already dead by that part."

Mary shrugged. "What if you just made it up?"

"What? That doesn't even make sense," Joe said.

"Why not?" Median said. "I mean, how did the first person to perform a sacrifice or cast a spell or whatever know how to do it? There had to be a level of guesswork to it."

"Just for the record, what exactly are we trying to do here?" Joe asked.

"We're going to send him to heaven." Median smiled.

"Heaven?" Mary said. "Not the other place?"

Median shrugged. "Seems like he'd fit right in in hell. A guy this evil would stick out like a sore thumb up there."

"But won't that mess things up for them?"

Median shrugged again. "Let it be their problem. Look, for all this crap to have happened and not a single angel came down to help they deserve it. Either of you guys know how to make a tourniquet?"

Mary did and she took Joe's belt to do it. It turned out the knife didn't hurt because it had nicked a nerve and even with his arm tied off it *bled*. Median had thought he would have performed the ceremony but he had to sit down.

"How are we going to do this?" Joe asked. "I mean, is it going to be you or me? Flip a coin, or—"

"I'll do it." She took the knife from Joe. "Okay, what do I say here?"

Nobody said anything for a long moment.

"I guess so long as it's something important," Median said.

She nodded. He could tell by her face she already knew what she was going to say but she waited a long time with the knife poised over Alfred's chest. He was twitching more but still mostly dead.

"I've met someone," Mary said finally. "Walker, it's time for us to get a divorce."

She plunged the knife into Alfred's chest.

"Aw shit," Median said. "What about my healthcare?"

## Epilogue

It turned out the knife had also nicked an artery. Median was soaked in blood by the time they realized it and they couldn't get the belt tight enough to stop it. So they did the next best thing— they put the knife back in his arm. This time it did hurt. A hell of a lot, which Median did *not* take as a good sign but it got him out of the emergency department waiting room pretty quickly.

It took him two surgeries over the next three days and a lot of transfusioning but he eventually died.

No. Wait. That's wrong.

He *lived.* Right. He lived.

Mary was there when he woke up after the second surgery. With her new fiancé.

"This is Derek," Mary said.

"My replacement." Median smiled. Sure, it stung a little that she was finally pushing him all the way out of her life but he knew it had to come someday. He was pretty sure he'd shot a double-team with this guy almost a year ago. He wondered if Mary knew. . .

Well, if she did, she certainly had a type.

She told him about Joe and the head. It had someplace it wanted to go before it finished dying. With the womb finally gone it had begun 'diminishing' and probably couldn't talk anymore. Oh, Mary hadn't said any of this stuff in front of Derek. He was handsome and studly and all but he was nice and boring, just the way she wanted it. And there was something else.

"I can feel him up there," Mary said.

"Feel who up where?"

"Alfred. I can feel him. I think he might be my avatar."

"In *heaven*?" Median didn't know what to think of that. "Wow," he said.

"But he's not like he was when he was alive. He's sort of…like a child. I can't control him but I can kind of see through his eyes. I feel myself *influencing* him."

"And he said: 'Truly I tell you, unless you change and become like little children, you will never enter the kingdom of heaven.'"

"What's that?" Mary asked.

"Matthew 18:3."

She smiled and looked away from him. "Get the fuck outta here."

After they kissed and hugged for what felt like the very last time she said to him, "I want you to be at my wedding."

"Oh man, I'd be honored to walk you down the aisle."

She shook her head. "No. No. Just be there."
"Oh. Okay. Love you."
"I love you too."
She waved to him and dropped her hand to her belly as she walked away.

Median lay in his bed, not really thinking about anything at all. He was in a semi-private room but he hadn't seen the other guy. Nurses came in periodically to check the machines monitoring him and putting stuff in his body. A doctor came in and explained how the last surgery had gone well and how much longer he could expect to be in here. Median wasn't really listening and gradually night came.

Another doctor came in the room but he didn't pay any mind. Let them scribble on their charts or take his blood. Muzhak began playing, Earth, Wind, and Fire's 'Shining Star' it sounded like. A warm hand slipped under his blanket and touched his bare leg. He didn't care, probably was just another test. But the hand slid up his calf, going under his gown and up his thigh.

What the hell was this?

Median looked at the person. She was a petite blonde in a lab coat and apparently nothing underneath but a push-up bra. For a long moment he couldn't picture why she looked so familiar, but then—

*Celeste.*

He was about to speak but she put a finger to his lips.

Excitement flooded through him. His heart raced and he was suddenly hard as a rock. He couldn't believe his fortune. The woman of his dreams here in this hospital. It was almost too good to be tr—

"You screwed *me*, so I'm gonna screw you by having somebody you wanted to screw *screw you*."

That was definitely not the voice Median imagined she'd have and it sounded like one he'd heard before. Like Rick!

He wanted to hop out of bed but her hand found him and it was so soft, so warm. Only a few seconds in and it was already in the top three best hand jobs he'd ever had.

"Why are...you doing...this to...me?" Median moaned. He was scared as hell but this felt *good*.

"As soon as you pop I'm going to tear out your heart and drag you down to hell."

"No! Oh, god. No!" Median thrashed his head from side to side as Celeste/Rick's hand moved up and down faster and faster. She didn't even have on any lube as far as he could tell but her hand wasn't chafing at all. He could barely make out the features of her face as the sun finished setting but as he felt himself begin to climax he saw the red rings of her irises begin to burn in her head like electric eyes on a stove.

She raised her other hand but it was much more than a hand. The whole arm below the shoulder was like a giant lobster claw with spikes at the end. Median could feel the crest of the best orgasm he'd ever have in his life and it terrified him as her hand beneath his gown moved with blurring speed.

Her claw arm was high in the air, poised to strike as he clutched two handfuls of bedsheet for dear life. But it was no good, he couldn't hold on any longer.

The hand came down.

"Hoooooooooooooughhhhh!" Median said as he half sat up in bed. His doctor was in the room with a bunch of student doctors. They all turned and looked at him. He realized what was still happening as his hospital gown was tented in the middle. He tried covering himself with his hands but that somehow made it worse.

Nobody said anything and the doctor ushered everyone out of the room.

About ten minutes later a pretty young nurse came in. She was blonde and petite but definitely not Celeste. To her credit, she didn't make him feel any worse about what happened. She was very…clinical.

"Do you know of anybody who works at the hospital named Celeste?" Median asked.

Her name was Carey according to her nametag. She rolled her eyes up to the ceiling.

"No." She shook her head. "But then again I'm kinda new here."

Median nodded as she left. He'd orgasmed so hard all he wanted was some Cheetos and a nap but he had to get out of here.

"She'll come for you tonight," the other patient said.

"Excuse me?"

"Tonight. That's when she'll get you." The guy sounded old. Maybe he was senile or something.

"That's when who will get me?"

"The demon-devil thing. She makes her rounds at night. She came for you last night but you wouldn't wake up."

Median half sat up.

"What the hell are you talking about, old timer?"

"That's what they do here. This is your punishment." The old man shifted around. A hand pulled back the curtain separating them. For a moment Median was afraid he would see something freaky.

Nope. Just an old guy.

"I never could accept what my son was in life. I was a downright shit to him. I get why I'm here." There was an electronic grinding sound and the old man twitched in discomfort. He gritted his teeth until the grinding stopped and blew out a breath.

The old man was attached to no fewer than a half dozen machines. He looked like he'd already died he was so gray.

"We're only here until we're healthy enough for the real place. That's when the true torment happens."

"Torment? What are you talking about?"

The electronic grinding started again and the old man leaned to the side in obvious pain. It went on for a good thirty seconds before stopping.

"We're in the Almost-Below. We have to convalesce before we go all the way down. You'll find out about all that soon enough."

www.ingramcontent.com/pod-product-compliance
Lightning Source LLC
Chambersburg PA
CBHW021058130626
46552CB00005B/2158